Deathwing over Veynaa

Douglas Hill is a Canadian who has lived in Britain for
several years. He became addicted to science fiction at an
early age – by reading comics like *Flash Gordon* – and has
remained a hopeless addict ever since. In the sixties he
began reviewing science fiction regularly for *Tribune*, at a
time when the national press barely acknowledged the
existence of sf. He is now Literary Editor of the *Tribune*,
has written many short stories and has compiled sf
anthologies.

Deathwing over Veynaa is the sequel to *Galactic Warlord*,
the first book about Keill Randor, the Last Legionary.

Also by Douglas Hill
in Piccolo
Galactic Warlord

Douglas Hill

Deathwing over Veynaa

Piccolo Books
in association with Victor Gollancz

First published 1980 by Victor Gollanz Ltd
This Piccolo edition published 1981 by Pan Books Ltd,
Cavaye Place, London SW10 9PG,
in association with Victor Gollanz Ltd
© Douglas Hill 1980
9 8 7 6 5 4 3
ISBN 0 330 26446 X
Printed and bound by
Hunt Barnard Printing Ltd, Aylesbury, Bucks

for Marilyn

part one

Rebels of the Cluster

chapter one

The watcher among the rocks had not noticed the point of light when it had first appeared, high in the pale yellow sky. Only when it had fallen further, enlarging, brightening, did the watcher's one huge eye glimpse it.

The watcher's six arms halted their activity. Within its cold brain messages were relayed and received. Silently it moved backwards, into a shadowed cleft among the rocks, its eye fixed unblinkingly on the hurtling object in the sky.

In seconds the object revealed itself as a metal capsule, man-sized and coffin-shaped. It fell bathed in fire as the atmosphere flared along its metal skin. And it fell with a high-pitched howl as its small retro rockets cut in, slowing its plunge – and at last depositing it with a bump and a slide among the rocks.

It was a standard escape capsule, in use on many of the spacecraft in the Inhabited Worlds. It had a tiny power supply, enough for some guidance control, for its retros and for a continuous 'Mayday' broadcast while in flight. It was a space-man's last resort when his ship was dangerously malfunctioning, beyond repair.

The capsule came to rest less than a hundred metres from the watcher. The great eye observed steadily as a seam opened in the capsule's hull, parting it into two halves. From within it, as if hatching from an egg, a spacesuited man emerged.

The man unfastened his helmet and took a deep, grateful breath of the cold air, then began to peel off the spacesuit, indifferent to the biting wind that swirled and moaned around him. He was a tall, lean young man with a strong-boned face, wearing what seemed to be a uniform – dark-grey tunic and close-fitting trousers tucked into boots. On the cuffs of the tunic were flashes and stripes of colour, and a sky-blue circlet decorated the upper chest. The same circlet appeared on the spacesuit helmet, and on the open and now useless capsule.

The man folded the spacesuit into a manageable bundle with the helmet and breathing pack, then straightened, studying his surroundings. It was an uninviting landscape of dark, bare rock, so ridged and creased and corrugated that, from above, it would look like badly crumpled cloth. Much of the rock was discoloured with broad smears of a substance that gleamed a sickly blue under the pale sun.

Yet, for all its dismal appearance, it was a place with an oxygen atmosphere, able to support human life – even if not comfortably. If the man from the capsule had been an ordinary spaceman, who had ejected from a crippled ship, he could have counted himself lucky.

But luck had nothing to do with it. His ship was intact – orbiting in deep space, under the guidance of the most unusual pilot in the Inhabited Worlds.

And the man from the capsule was no ordinary spaceman.

He was Keill Randor, the sole survivor of a race of people who had once been the galaxy's most renowned and most supremely skilled fighting force – the Legions of the planet Moros.

And he had chosen to land as he had done for a purpose – as part of a task he had to accomplish in this bleak place.

As his gaze swept across his surroundings, he caught a glint of metal deep in a shadowed cleft. He moved closer, warily – and saw the watcher.

And he knew that his task had begun.

The watcher was a robot – a work-robot, he recognized, probably with a limited programme and no decision faculties. Its body was wide and pyramid-shaped, with a low centre of gravity to keep it upright on rough terrain. It had six arms –

flexible, whippy tentacles of metal – with tools on their extremities, mining tools like drills, scoops, pincer-like grabs. Surmounting the body, some two metres from the ground, was a scanner 'eye' – which relayed pictures to screens that humans would monitor.

The robot moved slowly out from the shadow, rolling on heavy, rubbery treads that made its advance eerily silent.

Keill Randor stood still, watchful but relaxed, fairly sure that the heavy robot was no danger to him.

But he was less sure of his safety when, looking up, he saw two human figures who had appeared on a nearby rise, with old-fashioned laserifles held ready in their hands.

The smaller of the two figures waved an arm in a beckoning gesture. Keill gathered up his spacesuit and obeyed, moving with sure-footed, athletic speed up the uneven slope.

Both of the others wore hooded, one-piece coveralls, shiny and metallic, and probably thermally controlled. Garments like them were commonplace on many planets in the Inhabited Worlds. And the smaller of the two was a woman, for the coverall did nothing to hide the shapeliness of her figure – no more than it hid the bulk and muscle of her taller companion.

As Keill drew near, he saw an open, balloon-wheeled ground-car – of a make almost as out-of-date as the laserifles – standing a short distance beyond the two figures. He also saw the bulky man swing the rifle to fix its ugly muzzle on his chest.

But the woman merely looked him up and down, then nodded. She had large, dark eyes in a delicately oval face, but they held an expression of cool and competent authority.

'We picked up your mayday,' she said. 'My name's Joss – this is Groll.'

'Keill Randor. Thanks for coming out.' He glanced briefly at the rifle held by the bigger man. 'No need for that – I'm not armed.'

'Precautions,' the woman said. 'You've dropped into the middle of a war.'

'I know,' Keill said. 'That's why I'm here.' As the woman raised her eyebrows, he added, 'I heard some news about trouble here on the Cluster, and thought I could find work. But my ship's drive overloaded and I had to come the rest of the way in the capsule.'

The woman called Joss studied him curiously. 'Work? Are you some sort of soldier?'

'Some sort.'

'Mercenary!' spat the big man named Groll, a sneer on his coarse-featured face.

Keill looked at him coldly. 'Nothing wrong with being a mercenary – depending on who you fight for, and why.'

Groll was about to reply when the woman silenced him with a gesture. 'You'd better come and talk to the Council,' she said thoughtfully, motioning to the ground-car.

The vehicle was not only old-fashioned but old. Its drive stuttered and bellowed, its body rattled with every bump, and there was a bump every few centimetres. Conversation would have been impossible even if the biting wind had not snatched words away from mouths. So Keill sat back, staring out at the dismal vista of blue-smeared rock, wrapping himself in his thoughts.

He knew a good deal about this place where he had landed – more than he would admit to its people. He had come as prepared as possible, yet ahead of him remained a huge range of unknowns, of questions and mysteries. He would have to deal with them as they came up, while posing as a wrecked spaceman, a drifter, a soldier of fortune.

If they accepted him, his task would be that much easier. If not . . . then his ship and its strange pilot were near enough to scoop him up if he ran into dangers that even he could not overcome. So he was not alone.

Certainly not as alone as he once had been, totally, overwhelmingly, when he had learned that he was the only living remnant of an entire race of people. A race that had been deliberately, inhumanly, murdered.

At the time, he had not expected to feel that mind-numbing loneliness for long. The deadly radiation that had enveloped his world, the planet Moros, had brushed lightly against him, enough to plant a slow death within him. He had set out then, alone, with a steely determination, to use what time he had left to find out who had destroyed his world, and why.

But he had been diverted. And his life had been altered in ways that he would once have thought beyond belief.

He had been gathered up by a group of strange, elderly scientists, brilliant beyond the level of genius, whom he had come to know as the 'Overseers'. In their secret base, hidden within a small, uncharted asteroid, he had been cured of the radiation's lethal effects – and had learned the truth behind the murder of Moros.

The Overseers, tirelessly keeping watch over the Inhabited Worlds with uncanny monitoring devices, had discovered the existence of a mysterious being who was the single most malignant danger to the well-being of the unsuspecting galaxy. Knowing little else about this being – neither where, nor what, nor who he was – they had given him a name of their own: the Warlord.

But the Overseers at least knew the intentions of the Warlord. He was sending out emissaries and agents to spread the infection of war throughout the galaxy – to set nation against nation, race against race, planet against planet. Until, if he had his way, all the Inhabited Worlds would be ablaze with an ultimate war – and the Warlord would be waiting to emerge and rule whatever was left after that final catastrophe.

It was the Warlord, the Overseers were sure, who had destroyed Moros – before the Legions too could learn of his existence, and turn their might against him.

So the Overseers had sought and found Keill Randor, the

last legionary – and probably the most skilled fighting man in the galaxy, whether piloting his one-person space fighter or in individual, hand-to-hand combat. They wanted Keill to be *their* emissary – to go to worlds where they suspected the Warlord's influence was at work, and there to learn more about him and wherever possible to thwart his plans.

Keill had agreed – for the fight against the Warlord was *his* fight, too, against the murderer of Moros. But when he had left the secret asteroid to begin that fight, he had left considerably changed.

For one thing, the Overseers' scientific genius had not merely healed him of the radiation's effects. That deadliness had settled in Keill's bones – so the Overseers had *replaced* his entire skeletal structure, with a unique organic alloy. It was stronger and more resilient than even the toughest metal. As far as the most demanding tests showed, it was unbreakable.

And for another thing, his loneliness had ended. On the asteroid he had met an alien visitor – an intelligent being from another galaxy, for there were no intelligent life-forms other than man within the Inhabited Worlds.

Glr was the name of the alien, a female of a race called the Ehrlil – a race of long-lived explorers of the unfathomable intergalactic spaces, a race of small, winged beings who communicated telepathically. Glr herself, Keill soon found, had special qualities of her own – among them a boundless curiosity and an unquenchable sense of humour.

Glr became Keill's friend and companion when he left the Overseers' asteroid. Now she was at the controls of his ship, immensely distant, yet in contact with his mind through her telepathic power, which had no limits in space. She was also his only link with the Overseers – for they had kept the position of the asteroid a secret even from Keill, for fear that he might fall into the hands of their enemy, the Warlord, and be forced to betray them.

Keill and Glr had already had one encounter with forces of

the Warlord, and had defeated them. And in doing so Keill had learned a valuable fact. The Warlord's most important agents were organized into a special élite force, whose leader was known only as 'The One'. Many of its members came from the Altered Worlds, planets where mutations had taken place among the human inhabitants. But all of the members of that force, mutants or not, were skilled and powerful, and as malignantly evil as their Master. The nature of that force was revealed by its name – the Deathwing.

Beneath him, the ground-car's rumble altered, jolting Keill out of his memories. The big man called Groll, at the controls, had been guiding it through a winding series of gullies and low ravines. Now he had aimed it towards a low, flat slope, increasing its power. The wheels skidded slightly on the smeared blue substance, and Keill glanced down at it.

It was, he knew, a simple lichenous form of vegetation. It was also why he was there.

Because of that harmless lichen, war was brewing in this cold, rocky place. A war that showed all the signs of the insidious, poisonous influence of the Warlord.

Which meant that somewhere, sometime – perhaps very soon – Keill Randor would once again come face to face with the Deathwing.

The ground-car roared up to the top of the low ridge, and had begun its plunge down the far slope when Groll urgently brought it to a jerking, sliding halt.

Beyond the foot of the slope, from a broad, low area like a vast shallow basin within the rocks, rose a massive structure. It was cylindrical and flat-topped, resembling an enormous drum – some eight storeys high, with a frontage at least three hundred metres wide. Windows gleamed at regular intervals in its sturdy plasticrete walls, and at its base, between huge supporting buttresses, were wide openings that were more like loading bays than doorways.

On top of the building was a landing pad for spacecraft, on which was resting the bulbous oval shape of a cargo shuttle ship. Around the edge of the roof was a series of unsightly humps that Keill recognized as reinforced gun emplacements.

The weapons within them were heavy-duty laser cannon. And they were firing.

The building was under attack.

High in the yellow sky a silvery dart-shape veered and plunged. A one- or two-person fighter, Keill saw, with what seemed to be a skilled hand at the controls – and with more advanced weaponry than the out-dated lasers of the defenders. It was the crackling blast of an ion-energy gun that spat from the slender ship's nose as it dived towards the huge building.

Gobs of molten plasticrete exploded from the flat roof, within dangerous metres of the exposed shuttle ship. The silvery shape flashed over, curving and zig-zagging, while the laser cannon hissed and flared, the bright beams slashing in vain through the sky around the attacker.

Then the pilot of the gleaming ship pulled it around in a tight loop, on to a different course. Something had attracted his eye. Something like ... a ground-car in full view on a nearby rocky slope.

'Get out of here!' Keill shouted, as the slim, menacing shape arrowed towards them.

Groll dragged brutally at the car's controls, to force it back over the protecting lip of the ridge. But the elderly drive sputtered and hiccoughed, and the wheels slid beneath it.

Above them, the attacking ship swooped for the kill.

Groll yelled with fear, trying to scramble free of the car, ignoring Joss, who seemed frozen, unable to move.

But Keill Randor was a legionary of Moros – his reflexes, his muscles, his entire physique honed by a lifetime's training to a degree beyond most men's imagining.

In the fractional instant before flame blossomed from the ship's forward gun, he had grasped the back of Joss's coverall, braced himself, and flung her one-handed out of the open car, sprawling and tumbling down the slope, And in a follow-through to the same motion, he dived headlong after her.

Behind them, the entire slope seemed to erupt in a volcanic explosion of fire and shattered rock.

chapter two

The tumbling slide of Joss and Keill, over the greasy blue lichen, had ended in a shallow cleft in the rock – where they crouched while rock fragments, molten or splintered, hurtled around them. So they arose unharmed when the attacking ship had swept upwards after its pass at them and vanished.

Above them, the ground-car lay tilted crazily, the front end rearing up, crushed and smoking. The energy blast had struck just in front of it, but close enough to wreck it beyond repair – and to have killed any occupants.

Joss rubbed a grazed elbow, showing through a rent in her coverall's sleeve, and looked at Keill with new interest. 'Thanks for that. You're stronger than you look.'

Keill shrugged. 'It's more balance and leverage.'

'Perhaps. But I don't know many who could have done that.' She pointed up the slope. 'Not even him.'

Beyond the shattered car, the huge figure of Groll lay, stirring slightly. The force of the blast had flung him up the slope – but he had been far enough to one side to escape the full impact. As they watched, he struggled slowly to hands and knees, shaking his head dazedly.

Motioning to Keill, Joss started up the slope towards Groll – while in the distance, from the openings at the base of the mighty building, a crowd of people were surging out on to the rock.

In no time another ground-car had thundered up on to the slope and gathered them up. As they roared back down, Keill glanced over at Joss, seated beside him. Her hood had been pushed back, and her thick dark hair flowed free in the wind.

She seemed more excited than distressed by the narrow escape from danger – her eyes were sparkling, her fine-featured face glowing, and her smile as she turned towards Keill was radiant.

She leaned forward and put her lips to his ear. 'That's Home,' she shouted above the car's roar, pointing to the building that was looming ever closer. 'Where the Clusterfolk live.'

Keill blinked. 'All of them?'

'All.' She nodded, her smile widening. Keill grinned back in return – but the grin faded slightly when he caught the edge of a look from Groll, in the front seat. It was a look filled with a sullen, brooding dislike.

The big man had suffered no serious harm – but now he was clearly feeling that he had been shown up somehow, out on the slope. Keill sighed inwardly. Not an ideal start. Out of two people, he had made one friend, one enemy.

But, glancing at the lovely woman beside him, he was just as glad it hadn't worked out the other way round.

He settled back for the rest of the ride. As he did so, another thought formed within him. But it was not one of his own. It was the silent, inner voice of Glr, reaching into his mind.

I take it you are still alive, said the alien voice with an edge of sarcasm, *despite all the alarms I sensed in your mind just now.*

Keill began forming a silent reply, sorting through the events since his landing. He had no telepathic ability, but Glr could reach into his mind and pick up some of his thoughts.

More clarity, mudhead! scolded the inner voice.

Keill's mouth quirked in a private smile. For Glr, most human minds were too alien to read, too much a clutter of swirling, overlapping, jumbled thoughts and images – thick mud, Glr called it. She could read only surface thoughts and in only a few minds – those that could form their thoughts clearly and precisely, like unspoken words.

So Keill gathered his concentration, and related to Glr what had happened since his landing.

Then the war down there seems well under way, Glr commented when he was done.

'*So it seems,*' Keill agreed.

And you are still going to reveal yourself as a legionary?

'It's the best way, as I said before,' Keill replied. '*It should help to ease some suspicion.*'

But if there is a Deathwing agent there, Glr said worriedly, *you will be in grave danger from the outset.*

'*I've already been in danger,*' Keill said. '*I didn't come here to avoid danger.*'

He felt the ground-car slowing, and looked up to see that they were approaching one of the doorways at the base of the huge building. '*Enough for now – we've arrived.*'

Be wary, said Glr. Then her voice withdrew, as the car stopped.

The crowd surged forward round the vehicle, in a clamour of shouted concern and questions. As they climbed out of the car, Joss held up a hand, and the babble quietened.

'You'll hear all about it later,' she called. 'Right now the Council has to meet.'

'They're already gathered, Joss,' shouted a voice from among the throng. 'In the meetin' room.'

She waved her thanks with a smile, and Keill noted again the calm air of authority that she wore, and the admiring deference in the faces of the crowd around her – as obvious as the open curiosity with which they stared at him.

Then she was taking his arm and leading him through the crowd into the building, with Groll lumbering stolidly in their wake.

They entered a broad, low-ceilinged area where a number of other ground-cars were parked, with a few people and some of the six-armed work-robots moving among them. Beyond this area they passed through a doorway into a long, low brightly lit corridor, with more doorways and intersecting passages along its length.

The interior of the Home seemed cheerful but almost entirely functional, the bright plastic of its walls only rarely interrupted by metal or ceramic designs. And the people that Keill glimpsed through the doorways, or passed in the corridor, seemed equally functional in their shiny coveralls – though all had time to call a friendly greeting to Joss, and to peer curiously at Keill.

'How many are there?' Keill asked.

'The Clusterfolk? Six hundred and forty-one.'

'Make it forty-two,' Keill said, and was pleased when her smile glinted.

But it seemed a laughably small number of people, he thought, to go to war against a world.

At the corridor's end they stepped on to a moving walkway, rising upwards, twining round a descending walkway to make a double spiral. It took them rapidly up to the topmost level, where they followed another broad corridor to its end. Gleaming metal double doors stood closed before them.

Joss let her hand rest lightly on Keill's arm. 'Will you wait here while I speak with the Council? Just a few moments. And Groll—' she glanced at the big man '—you too.'

'Are you a Councillor?' Keill asked her.

'One of several. You'll meet them.' Her smile flashed, and she turned away.

When the double doors had closed behind her Keill leaned back against the wall of the corridor, patient, relaxed. He knew that Groll was glowering in his direction, and had no doubt that the big man had something to say. He did not have to wait long.

'Reckon you're a spy, that's what,' Groll rumbled aggressively. 'Dirty Veynaan spy.'

Keill said nothing. Veynaa, he knew, was the large neighbouring planet on which the Cluster's six hundred folk had declared war. It was not surprising that a Clusterman might be wary of spies. Or perhaps Groll merely had an ignorant man's aversion to strangers.

Then again, there might be something more to the big man's hostility. Something deeper and more deadly. It might be worthwhile, Keill thought, to stir him up a little and see what emerged.

'Got nothin' to say?' Groll sneered, stepping closer.

Keill looked at him without expression. 'I'll say this,' he replied flatly. 'You've managed something I didn't think possible.'

A puzzled frown wrinkled Groll's brow. 'Whassat?' he demanded suspiciously.

'To be even stupider than you look.'

Groll was fairly fast for a man of his bulk. His knotted fist swung without warning in a savage, clubbing punch.

It was a grave mistake – but Groll did not have time to realize it. He did not even have time to register that the punch had missed, that Keill had swayed aside just far enough.

Then Keill struck him, twice, his hands blurring past any eye's ability to follow their speed. He struck with fingertips only, not wishing to kill, the fingers of one hand jabbing deep into Groll's bulging belly, those of the other hand driving into the small of Groll's back as the first blow doubled him over. The second impact and Groll's own impetus sent the big man lurching forward, his head meeting the hard plastic wall with a meaty thud.

As the unconscious bulk of Groll slid to the floor, a sound behind Keill brought his head round. Joss was standing framed in the open double doors, staring wide-eyed.

'Sorry,' Keill said. 'He got a little . . . aggressive.'

'He usually does.' For all her surprise, she did not seem perturbed, Keill saw, and she hardly spared a glance for the fallen Groll. 'You're a very unusual man. I could barely see you move.'

Keill waited, saying nothing.

She smiled quickly, stepping aside. 'You'd better come and meet the others.'

The room beyond the doors was sizeable, but no less functional than the other parts of the building Keill had seen. It was dominated by a long, low table, behind which stood a few metal cabinets and some standard equipment including a computer outlet and a holo-tape viewer. But Keill's attention was on the four people at the table.

Two were older men, grey-haired and stringy. A third was an equally grey-haired woman, but heavy-bodied, with a cheerful ruddy face and bright eyes. The fourth was a younger man, tall, dark-haired, with a narrow intense face. They all wore variants of the shiny coverall favoured by the Cluster-folk; there were no signs of rank or authority.

'The Council of the Cluster,' Joss said formally as they approached the table. 'This is Shalet, Council leader,' she went on, indicating the big grey-haired woman. 'This is Fillon.' The young, thin-faced man. 'And this is Bennen, and Rint.' The two older men.

Keill nodded to them all agreeably, but had not missed the subtle ordering of the introductions. It was the leader, Shalet, and Fillon who – besides Joss herself – were the important members of this Council.

There was a brief silence while the five inspected Keill and he studied them. Keill broke it first. 'I'm Keill Randor. Joss will have told you how I came here, and why I was coming in the first place.'

'She did,' Shalet replied in a resonant baritone. 'Says you're a professional soldier.'

Keill smiled wryly. 'Mercenary was Groll's word.'

Shalet shrugged beefy shoulders. 'Don't matter. Joss says you're pretty good. Saved her life – we got to thank you for that.'

'And Groll just found out,' Joss put in, 'how good he is.'

One of the old men leaned forward. 'Y' mean big Groll got nasty, and you're still standin'?' He shook his head wonderingly. 'You're more'n pretty good, boy.'

'Where'd you learn soldierin'?' Shalet asked.

Keill had been expecting the question. 'On the planet Moros,' he said levelly.

Above the mutters of surprise, Fillon's snort of derision rang out. 'The Legions?' There was an edge of a sneer on the narrow face. 'They died out, not so long ago. Everybody knows that.'

'Perhaps some survived,' Joss said softly.

'One did, anyway,' Keill said. He slipped a hand into his tunic, and took out a disc fastened to a thin chain. Around the edge of the disc was the same blue circlet as on his uniform, and within the ring of blue was a tiny, colour holo-pic of Keill's face, with details of his name and rank, embedded deep in the plastic. 'This is a Legion ID, if it means anything to you.'

'Does to me, boy,' said the older man named Rint. 'Seen 'em before, on the vid. Uniform too, now I recollect.'

Fillon snorted again. 'So you're a legionary turned mercenary?'

'My people are dead, and I have to earn my keep,' Keill said quietly. 'It's the only work I know.'

'And how do we know,' Fillon snapped, 'that you didn't hire out to Veynaa, first?'

Keill allowed a puzzled expression to form on his face, and Shalet saw it. 'Veynaa's the planet we're at war with,' she explained. Then she turned impatiently to Fillon. 'And you know better'n that about the Legions. Never fought in an unjust war. If they was around, they'd likely fight for *us*, if we could afford 'em. Spyin' wasn't their trade, neither.'

'It still isn't,' Keill said firmly.

'I'll need more than words,' Fillon sneered, 'to convince me.'

Shalet slapped a broad hand on the table. 'Not me! I get a good feeling from you, Randor. Reckon the Cluster could do with a fightin' man like you.'

'Don't be naive,' Fillon objected. 'He could be dangerous!'

''Course he could!' Shalet boomed. 'If he's the only legionary left, maybe he's the most dangerous man around! So let him join us, an' be dangerous to Veynaa! We can tell 'em we got *two* weapons . . .'

'Shalet!' Joss broke in sharply.

'Oh, right – sorry.' Shalet subsided. 'Anyway, what's the decision?'

Fillon stood up abruptly, eyes burning. 'I tell you this man should be kept under guard, till we're sure of him!'

'An' how're we gonna be sure?' Shalet asked.

'Wait till Quern gets back!' Fillon snapped. 'Quern will know.'

The others all began talking at once, but Joss's clear voice sliced through the hubbub. 'If Keill Randor had been locked up earlier today,' she said, 'I would be dead.'

'True enough,' Shalet agreed. 'But maybe Fillon's got a point. Wouldn't hurt to wait till Quern can have a talk with him.' She glanced around, the two old men nodding in agreement. 'Right – let's be fair. Randor, I don't think myself you got anythin' t' do with Veynaa, but we can't take chances. You can be free to come and go as you like around the Home, but there's gotta be someone with you all the time. An' we'll talk about it again when Quern's back. All right?'

Keill glanced at Joss, who looked sympathetic, then at Fillon, who looked annoyed. 'If that's what you want,' he said calmly.

'Reckon it won't be so bad,' Shalet added with a broad grin, 'if Joss volunteers to keep an eye on y'.'

'I will,' Joss said readily. Then she grimaced down at her torn coverall. 'But first I need to change.'

'Then while Joss is prettyin' herself,' Shalet chortled, 'you come on with me, Randor. I'll give you a personal guided tour of the Home.'

She clapped a powerful hand on Keill's shoulder and propelled him towards the door, talking boisterously. But Keill's mind was still fixed on the words that the big woman had spoken earlier – words charged with menace.

Two weapons . . .

chapter three

On their way through the doors, Keill saw that the corridor was empty, which meant either that Groll had recovered or that he had been carried elsewhere. In either case, Keill knew, he had stored up trouble for himself from that source. Not that one more bit of trouble, he thought, would make much difference.

Preoccupied with such thoughts he walked with Shalet back towards the moving walkway and down to the lower levels. So he was only half-hearing her voluble stream of information – much of which he had learned earlier from the Overseers, while preparing for his mission.

Shalet had begun with the basic fact that the small planet on which they stood was the largest body of a collection of planetoids, asteroids and bits of space rubble which had been drawn by various cosmic forces to cling together, so that the whole came to be called the Cluster.

It moved through space as a single object, rotating round a common axis. And the larger bodies had, over the millennia, developed simple forms of life, mostly various lichenous growths including the blue substance Keill had seen, and a thin but breathable atmosphere.

The Cluster orbited its sun quite near, in astronomical terms, to a larger planet. When mankind's early starships had brought colonists to this system – during the ancient Millennium of the Scattering which had spread man through the galaxy – they had found the large planet, which they named Veynaa, suitable in every way to support human life.

They also explored the Cluster thoroughly – with one priceless result. A scientist, named Ossid, studying the blue lichen, found it to be a rich source of an amazingly broad-spectrum antibiotic – which the Veynaan colonists named *ossidin* after its discoverer.

So the colony's fortune was made. In the centuries after the Scattering, when the colonized planets were forming contacts, trading links and so on, ossidin proved a valuable resource. The Veynaans planted a small sub-colony of workers on the Cluster to gather the lichen and ship it back to Veynaa for processing. And Veynaa prospered hugely on the ossidin trade.

Eventually, though, the people of the Cluster – never more than a few hundred – stopped thinking of themselves as Veynaans. They enlarged their central base into the present massive structure, named it Home, and called themselves Clusterfolk. And a time came when those tough and in-dependent-minded men and women wanted to break free of Veynaan control. They wanted to govern themselves, and to take a fairer share of the rich profits from the ossidin trade.

When the Veynaans refused, anger and unrest swept the Cluster. Relations grew more bitter when the Clusterfolk went on strike, refusing to ship ossidin. A few violent attacks on visiting Veynaan officials were followed by retaliatory raids. Unrest became rebellion.

Then recently, without warning, the Clusterfolk had issued a threat. If their independence was not granted, they said, they would declare war on Veynaa.

At this point Keill restored his full attention to Shalet, since the war was why he was there. Shalet went on to say that, for a while, Veynaa had been leaving the Cluster mostly alone – except for occasional overflights and minor harassments by Veynaan ships, like the one Keill had run into that day.

'They think it's comical,' the big woman grumbled, 'us folk declarin' war on them. They figure it's just a lotta noise, an' we'll come to our senses soon.'

'Still,' Keill said carefully, 'it does seem a fairly unequal fight.'

'Sure it does.' Shalet set her jaw. 'But not if we've got ourselves an equalizer.'

'Is that what you hinted at before?' Keill asked, trying to sound casual. 'Some weapon?'

'Somethin' like that. But I shouldn't be talkin' about it. I'll leave it to Quern to tell y' about it, when he figures it's all right.'

Keill paused for a moment, so as not to seem too eagerly curious. 'This Quern sounds important.'

'He is,' Shalet assured him. 'Been a big help to us ever since he came. Gonna win this war for us, Quern is.'

A premonition stirred behind Keill's calm control. 'Since he came? He's not from the Cluster?'

'Nope – offworlder, like you,' Shalet grinned.

'I got the impression,' Keill said lightly, 'that some Clusterfolk don't like offworlders too well.'

Shalet snorted. 'Don't judge the Cluster from the likes of Groll, or Fillon. Lots of folk here are from offworld, come to get work before the trouble started. Must be a hundred or so.' Her laugh boomed. 'Fillon himself, he's one of 'em, an' Joss too. All good Clusterfolk, now – even if Fillon gets a bit prickly sometimes.'

Keill nodded, storing the information away. It was an interesting fact about Fillon, though not fully explaining the young man's hostility to Keill. And the mystery man Quern was even more interesting . . .

But he knew better than to arouse suspicion by pressing Shalet with even more questions. He regained his expression of polite interest as the guided tour continued.

They descended at first to the lowest levels of the great structure, where Shalet led him through the sizeable areas where much of the work of the Home went on. Keill watched the work-robots disgorge their heaps of fragmented, lichen-covered rock, which were gathered up to be powdered in mighty machines and packed into storage containers.

Shalet explained that the Cluster was stockpiling the raw ossidin, while the rebellion continued. 'When we're free,' she said, 'we'll get the stuff processed offplanet, and market it ourselves. An' we'll get some new equipment – not all this out-of-date stuff the Veynaans put on us. Quern's makin' all the arrangements.'

'He seems to know his way around,' Keill commented.

'Quern's been a trader all over the galaxy,' Shalet said proudly. 'Knows more about trade than any of us.'

Keill nodded, making no further comment, but adding another fragment to the mystery of Quern.

Shalet went on to describe the shipping process. An elevator, rising in a huge vertical shaft up through the Home, lifted the containers of raw ossidin to the roof, to be loaded on to the shuttles.

'You said shuttles,' Keill put in. 'I saw only one.'

'There're two – but Quern's got the other one. Makin' a trip,' Shalet said vaguely.

The shuttles, she continued, carried the containers up to a giant ultrafreighter, in a parking orbit round the Cluster. And when it was fully loaded, it transported the raw ossidin to be processed – to Veynaa, before the rebellion.

More information for Keill to tuck away. He knew something of the enormous interplanetary ultrafreighters – ten times as long as his own spaceship, and proportionately as wide. It seemed that the Cluster had everything they needed for running the ossidin trade – once they had gained their independence.

Farther on among the lower levels, Shalet took him through maintenance areas, workshops, laboratories, clerical rooms and more. All of these areas were swarming with busy Clusterfolk and their robots. And everyone had a cheery greeting for Shalet, and took time also for a careful look at

Keill, accompanied often enough by a friendly nod. Keill smiled to himself at the buzz of talk that arose in their wake as they continued – talk in which he could hear the word 'legionary'. News never travels faster, he thought, than in a closed community.

On another level they glanced into a chamber full of huge tanks that produced the basics of the Home's food.

'Food's mostly recycled and synthetic,' Shalet remarked, 'but it keeps the belly full – and keeps us goin' since Veynaa cut off supplies. There's water under the rock outside so we could last a couple more years, if we needed, on our own.'

'But you won't need to?' Keill asked.

'Uh-uh. We're gonna finish off the Veynaans quick.'

The words seemed all the more chilling for being spoken so casually. Of course it might just have been a figure of speech, Keill knew. But he wondered . . .

The upper levels of the enormous honeycombed building held a variety of communal rooms – recreation rooms, eating areas and sleeping quarters; the last ranging from sizeable apartments for families to tiny one-person cubicles. The tour ended in front of the narrow door to one of these cubicles. It offered little more than a narrow bunk and storage niches, with a slit of window in one wall.

'This can be yours,' Shalet said. 'Ain't much, maybe, but at least the singles get a place of their own. Privacy's a luxury in a place like this.'

Keill agreed, gratefully, knowing how he would have been limited if he had had to share accommodation with several curious Clusterfolk.

'Showers an' so on are along there,' Shalet added, pointing. 'An' we eat pretty soon. Someone'll come an' show you, but I reckon you're all right on your own till then. Stay put, though, don't want to upset Fillon by wanderin' round alone, do y'?'

She grinned, and turned away.

Keill sank thankfully on to the hard bunk, glad for the chance to digest all that he had learned that day, to examine it for facts that related to his purpose on the Cluster. The window-slit showed that, outside, night had fallen – so it had been a long day, as well as an active one.

And it had been mostly enjoyable. The Clusterfolk were likeable, good people – Keill had considerable respect for their sturdy, hard-working, determined approach to life. But with the respect came sadness. Normally, they would have little chance of carrying through their impossible dream of independence. They were too few and Veynaa was too strong.

How could six hundred people with laserifles and two cargo shuttles fight a whole world? When Veynaa finally decided to squash their rebellion, the end of the Cluster's dream would be tragic – and calamitous.

Yet Shalet had let those hints slip – of a weapon, an 'equalizer', and finishing the Veynaans off.

In the midst of those disturbing thoughts, Glr slipped into Keill's mind. And she seemed no less disturbed, when Keill told her what Shalet had been saying.

It all forms a most unpleasant equation, she said. *With a weapon, and a human called Quern, as the unknown factors.*

'I'll find out more,' Keill assured her. 'But I need to be careful about asking questions.'

True. But time is short.

'This Quern will return to the Cluster sometime,' Keill replied. 'I'll surely learn more then.'

It will be an interesting meeting, Glr commented.

Keill caught the hint of anxiety in the alien's inner voice. '*About Quern – are you thinking what I'm thinking?*'

Indeed – literally so, at this moment. There was a trace of Glr's laughter, quickly fading. *Certainly he follows the pattern. An outsider, gaining a position of influence and power, guiding the people around him to accelerate the progress towards war. There can be little doubt.*

'*Deathwing.*' The word resounded hollowly within Keill's mind.

It is the way that the Warlord works, Glr agreed. *And it seems we have come none too soon.*

Keill was silent for a moment, weighing the grim conclusion. Before he could reply, there was a subdued tap at the door of his cubicle. He felt Glr slip out of his mind as he moved to the door.

Joss was standing there, looking restored and lovely, her smile warm.

'Hungry?' she said. 'The food hall is serving in a few minutes.'

'Starving,' Keill said truthfully, returning her smile.

The food hall's plain, functional plastic tables and stools were crowded when they reached it. Keill followed Joss's slender form through the throng, to the central automated counter where they collected their meals in closed containers. As they found a table, Keill saw Shalet across the room, who gave him a wave and a broad wink.

Joss laughed. 'I hope Shalet's tour didn't weary you.'

'Not for a minute,' Keill said. 'Very informative.' Catching Joss's quick glance, he smiled and added, 'Don't worry, she didn't spill any secrets.'

'There's a saying in the Home,' Joss said wryly. 'A secret can be kept for five minutes – an important secret for half as long.'

Keill chuckled. 'And will a time come,' he asked lightly, 'when I can be trusted with Cluster secrets?'

'Oh yes, soon,' Joss said. 'The folk have accepted you already. They're delighted to have a legionary on their side.'

'Not all of them,' Keill said. He had caught sight of the bulky form of Groll, in a far corner, glowering darkly under a livid bruise on his forehead.

Joss followed his gaze. 'Groll won't forget what you did to him,' she warned.

Keill shrugged. 'Tell him to keep his fighting for the Veynaans.'

The conversation declined a little as they turned to their meal. Shalet had been right, Keill found, eating in the Home was more like refuelling than enjoyment. But fuel was necessary, and he dutifully worked his way through what was before him.

When they had done, Joss looked up, hesitating a moment. 'Would you like to walk awhile,' she said tentatively, 'if you're not tired?'

'I'd like to,' Keill said quickly. 'But won't you get bored with keeping watch on me?'

Joss laughed softly. 'I'm not. Whatever Fillon says, I don't think you need to be watched.'

Keill felt pleased at the implication that she was there for his company, not for security reasons, and even more pleased when she calmly and naturally slipped her arm into his.

They strolled the corridors awhile, talking – or at least Keill was talking, for Joss was a superb listener, attentive and responsive. She seemed especially fascinated by Keill's life as a legionary, and it was a subject he was happy to talk about – up to a point. While tales of past adventures with the Legions were one thing, he had to be vague and evasive when Joss sought to know more about what he had been doing since the destruction of Moros. Secrets, he thought darkly, on both sides. But he knew it could not be otherwise.

Eventually they made their way to one of the small recreation rooms. A broad window occupied much of one wall, and Joss led him to it, to gaze out in silence at the star-brilliant night. It was an impressive view, Keill admitted. The starlight glinting on the stark and rugged rock slopes around the Home gave them a delicate, eerie beauty.

Joss lifted a slim finger to point at the sky, where one fat golden spot of light stood out, smaller than a moon but larger than any of the stars.

'Veynaa,' she said quietly.

As Keill obediently looked a voice from the doorway broke in. 'Joss?'

Keill turned to see an anxious-looking Clusterman hurrying towards them, bending to mutter something in Joss's ear.

She looked at Keill regretfully. 'I'm sorry. I must go.'

'Trouble?' he asked.

'No – just the opposite. I'll tell you tomorrow, if I can.'

'Are you going to let me find my way back, unguarded?' Keill grinned.

She laughed. 'As long as you don't get lost.'

Keill returned to his cubicle directly. Wandering around alone would be pointless, he decided – it might reawaken suspicion, and he did not yet know where to begin searching for answers to his questions. In any case, he realized, it had been quite a day, and the thought even of the hard bunk in his cubicle was appealing.

But as he reached it, Glr's inner voice spoke to him, laughter bubbling behind the silent words.

I have always wondered about human courting rituals, she teased. *They seem more dull than those of my race.*

'If I ever do any courting, as you call it,' Keill replied, '*you can stay out of my head.*'

Willingly, Glr laughed. *But one day I must tell you about the mating flights of the Ehrlil.*

'*Can we change the subject?*' Keill said sourly. '*I'm sleepy.*'

Before you sleep, Glr said more soberly, *you might want to know that your ship's sensors have detected a spacecraft nearby, on a course for the Cluster.*

Keill sat up quickly. '*Any identification?*'

Not yet. But it will soon be near enough for more accurate scanning.

'*It might be another Veynaan raider,*' Keill said. '*But it could also be . . .*'

The mysterious Quern, Glr put in. *Wait, now – the ship is closer. It has . . .* She seemed to hesitate.

'*It has what?*' Keill asked.

Glr did not reply.

'*What is it?*' Keill asked, puzzled.

Silence.

'*Glr?*' Unease trailed a cold finger down Keill's spine. Gathering his concentration, he formed the mental words with the utmost care. '*Glr – are you reading me?*'

Silence still – as empty and total as the silence of infinite space.

Communication had been cut off. And, since Glr was the communicator, that meant only one thing.

Something – far out in the depths of space, unknowable to Keill, beyond any guessing – had happened to Glr.

chapter four

Keill did not sleep that night. He spent much of it staring out of the window-slit, at the star-stippled depths that concealed his ship, far beyond the range of human vision. Tension and anxiety seethed behind his iron control, and his imagination went into over-drive.

Perhaps a real malfunction had developed in his ship, he thought. Or perhaps Glr's telepathic power – still mostly a mystery to Keill – had failed her. Or, again, perhaps that incoming spacecraft had been a Veynaan raider after all, who had spotted Glr and attacked.

Keill did not even let himself think about the chance that the strange ship might well have been carrying the man called Quern and that *he*, for some unknown reason, might have attacked Glr.

Throughout the long night, he regularly formed the inner mental call to Glr. As regularly, no response came to break the silence. For a wild moment he thought of stealing the remaining shuttle from the roof of the Home and hurtling out to where Glr had been orbiting. But that would finish his mission on the Cluster before it had started. And Glr would not want that, even if she was . . .

He could not bring himself to confront the word. Instead, he clung to the possibility that there was some simple explanation for Glr's silence. And, since there was nothing else to do, he waited.

It was a basic element in every legionary's training. When waiting was necessary, you waited – calmly, patiently, uncomplainingly.

And you remained alert, ready at all times for the moment that put an end to waiting.

When Joss appeared at Keill's door in the morning, he greeted her with relaxed calm, showing no signs of his night-long turmoil. Nor did he fail to notice a difference in her – a suppressed excitement, shining in the depths of her large eyes. Somehow, on this morning, Keill doubted whether it had anything to do with him.

'Come and eat with me,' Joss said brightly. 'The Council's meeting early today, and they want you there.'

Keill raised his eyebrows. 'Again? Why?'

Her excitement threatened to burst its restraints. 'Quern's back.'

'Is he?' More anxiety clamoured behind the barrier of Keill's control. So the strange ship last night had been Quern's. Then Glr could be . . .

But again he pushed that thought away. If Quern was what Keill thought he was, every fragment of his alertness and wariness would be needed in that confrontation. 'Let's not keep him waiting, then,' he said, with a convincingly light-hearted smile.

They made short work of breakfast, no more tasty than the previous evening's meal, and were soon entering the heavy double doors of the meeting room. The Council was seated as before, at the long table, and Keill again stood facing them as Joss slipped into her place. He nodded his greetings to Shalet and the two old men, let his glance slide easily across Fillon's chill scowl, then focused his attention on the stranger seated in their midst.

The man was tall, taller even than Keill, but unnaturally, skeletally thin, fleshless skin drawn tightly over the jutting bones of his face. He wore a high-collared, loose tunic with flowing sleeves, almost a short robe, loose-fitting trousers and light shoes like slippers on his long feet. The clothing was bright and colourful – incongruously so, for the man was an albino. His skin was an unrelieved, corpse-like white – and white, too, was the thinning hair that straggled nearly to shoulder-length. Yet Keill guessed that the man was only in early middle age – his movements were brisk, his back martially straight.

The albino examined Keill silently for a moment. And Keill noted a flicker of something like puzzlement, even unease, within the unpleasantly red-rimmed eyes in their deep, bony sockets.

'A legionary, I am told?' the man said at last, his voice as colourless as his skin.

'Keill Randor.' Keill kept his own voice and face expressionless, standing relaxed and still, though the adrenalin was surging in his veins.

'You are fortunate to have survived the end of your world,' the cold voice said. Another flicker showed in the red eyes. 'Were there other survivors?'

'There may have been.'

'Ah. Presumably then you have not encountered any. How tragic.' The words were spoken with a total absence of feeling. 'I am Quern, as you will know.' The albino paused, but Keill said nothing. 'I have been told of the ... interesting way you came among us. And of how ... keen you are to join the Cluster's fight against oppression.'

Again the words sounded false, unnatural, in that dead voice. Again Keill made no reply, but his eyes locked with the red-gleaming eyes of Quern.

And he knew – instinctively, but beyond any doubt – that he was looking into the eyes of the Deathwing.

'Are you not going to answer?' Quern asked.

'I wasn't aware you had asked a question,' Keill said calmly.

He saw that the others were looking at one another, worried by the hostility that had appeared between the two men. Joss especially looked upset – but then relieved when Quern uttered a short, barking laugh.

'Good. At least you are not pouring out assurances of how devoted you are to our cause.'

Keill's expression did not change. 'I came to offer my services as a soldier. I'm still finding out about your cause.'

'Indeed. And your services will be welcome.' The albino's thin lips twisted in a half-smile. 'We would not be so unwise as to reject a legionary. Even though some of us—' he waved a bony hand towards the still scowling Fillon '—are still a trifle unsure of your . . . trustworthiness.'

'I'd be glad,' Keill said dryly, 'if you could suggest how I might prove myself trustworthy.'

'So speaks a man of action.' Quern's sardonic smile broadened. 'And I shall do just that. There is a task which you can perform for us – after which, if it is completed properly, we will be satisfied.'

'Name it,' Keill said curtly.

'At the suitable time,' Quern replied. 'There are preparations to be made and I must soon leave the Cluster again, briefly. When I return, all will be made clear. Until then—' he raised a long white finger, for emphasis '—I must ask you to continue to restrict your movements, and remain within the Home. The outside areas, including the roof, must be off limits.'

Keill shrugged. 'As you wish.'

'Excellent.' The red eyes flicked towards Joss, a gleam of malicious laughter within them. 'I'm sure that restriction will not prevent you from . . . occupying yourself pleasurably.'

As he spoke he rose to his feet, making clear that the meeting had ended. Keill turned to the door with the others, and Joss moved to join him. They walked together wordlessly for a while, Keill wrapped in thought, Joss glancing at him concernedly now and then.

Finally she broke the silence. 'Quern's an unusual person,' she said, almost defensively.

'He is,' Keill agreed wryly. 'Unusual.'

'He upsets people sometimes,' Joss went on quickly. 'He can seem strange, unpleasant. But he's completely dedicated to the Cluster. And he says there's no room in a war like ours for . . . finer feelings. We need to be hard, ruthless, single-minded – ready to make any sacrifice.'

Keill shook his head wearily. 'I've heard many military leaders say the same thing. That only victory is important, no matter how it's achieved.'

'You sound disapproving,' Joss replied. 'But we have no choice. Against an enemy as powerful as Veynaa, we must fight any way we can.'

'My people believed,' Keill said, 'that if you sacrifice everything to win – all principles, all sense of right – you end up with a pretty hollow victory. There's a line in a Legion song – better to lose like men than win like beasts.'

'But the Legions never lost,' Joss murmured.

'They lost, and they died, in a war they didn't know they were fighting,' Keill said harshly. 'Against an enemy who knew all about single-minded ruthlessness – and worse.'

Joss looked up at him, her eyes dark and clouded. 'I'm sorry.'

'Don't be.' Keill gathered his control, forced a half-smile. 'I'm a little edgy, that's all. It's being kept in the dark about everything – including now this task Quern has in mind for me.'

'Don't worry,' Joss assured him. 'You'll know what's happening soon. Just wait a while.'

'Of course,' Keill replied flatly. 'I'll wait.'

Two days of waiting later, even Keill's patience was wearing thin, his trained control fraying at the edges.

Nothing had happened in that time that furthered his mission, or that answered any of his questions.

He had not seen Quern again, nor heard anything more from him.

And, worse, a deathly silence had remained the only response to all of his mental calls to Glr.

Of course his days had not been entirely empty. He had continued to see much of Joss, when she was not occupied with Quern and the Council. They ate together, strolled the corridors, chatted to other Clusterfolk, watched occasional old holo-tapes. Once they had visited the gymnasium to play an intricate variation of hand-ball that was popular in the Home. Keill, with his legionary's reflexes, had eventually won – but Joss had proved lithe, athletic and astonishingly quick.

To an outsider, then, they would have seemed like any young man and woman who enjoyed being together. And Keill might have been happy during those days – had he not carried within him a storm of frustration and anxiety.

It was even worse during those hours when Joss left him to his own devices, and when everyone in the Home seemed to have something to do except him. Then he would wander the corridors and walkways, or more often sit at a window – in his cubicle or in a recreation room – brooding over the bleak landscape of the Cluster, or at night staring ever more despairingly at the starry expanses of sky.

Late in the afternoon of the third day, he was in his cubicle when the walls trembled minutely with a distant, rumbling vibration. For an instant he wondered if another Veynaan raider had swooped down on the Home. But when the sound was not repeated, he guessed its real cause.

One of the shuttles had lifted off from the pad on the building's roof.

And Quern had said he was leaving again, briefly.

A thought that had been germinating in the back of his mind flowered suddenly. He remembered Quern's words, when the albino had confirmed the restrictions on Keill's movements. The outside of the Home was off limits – especially the *roof*.

So possibly something was up there that Keill was particularly not allowed to see. And possibly it was still there, though Quern was absent.

If he could get on to the roof unseen – at night . . . At least, he thought sourly, it would be something to do. Aside from going insane with waiting.

On the very heels of that thought came another.

But this time – not his own.

Keill. I am here.

He sprang up with a shout, relief and gratitude flooding through him like a tide.

'Glr! What happened? Where have you been?'

I have had to be silent, Glr replied, *and later I will have to be silent again. The human called Quern is an extremely powerful short-range telepath.*

Keill sat down again slowly, unnerved by the grave tone of Glr's mental voice. '*I don't understand.*'

I became aware of his power only when his ship entered the Cluster's atmosphere, Glr replied, *because his mental reach is limited. But then I had to shield my mind at once – and yours as well. And communication is impossible through a shield.*

Chill realization struck Keill of what it would have meant – to the Overseers' secrecy, to his own chances – if Quern had freely been able to read his mind. 'So he must be from the Deathwing. And from one of the Altered Worlds – a mutant.'

Without doubt.

'But aren't you in danger?' Keill asked.

I do not think he is aware of me. I touched his mind only for an instant – and my mind may be too alien for him to have recognized the touch, or my shield. But he is aware of your shielding, and is puzzled by it. He probably believes it is a natural barrier. And he has probed and struck at it many times.

'Struck? I felt nothing.'

You are not a telepath, Glr said. *But to another telepath, a mind-blow can be as violent and painful as a physical blow. And within his limits, Quern's power is enormous. I feel – battered.*

Only then, guiltily, did Keill become aware of the intense weariness that lay behind Glr's words.

'I'm sorry. How can I help?'

You cannot. I will rest soon – and hope that his next visit is as brief as this one. But the Overseers are worried – for Quern will certainly have informed the Deathwing of his encounter with a legionary.

Keill nodded. The only other member of the Deathwing he had met had had no chance to communicate with his leader – the nameless 'One' – before he met his death at Keill's hands. But now. . .

'Does it matter? Quern has no reason to think I'm anything other than I seem to be – a surviving legionary turned drifter.'

Perhaps. But the Deathwing, as you know, does not always act reasonably. And I believe that Quern is particularly unbalanced – his mind is repulsive. Glr's voice was sharp with distaste. *It may be a cause of his heightened power. You must take extreme care, Keill. And we will not be able to speak when Quern is on the Cluster.*

'I understand,' Keill said grimly. 'Let me tell you now what's been happening. And one other thing – while Quern's away, I'm going to have a look up on that roof. Tonight.'

part two

Betrayal in space

chapter five

Keill stepped out of his cubicle into the deserted corridor. The night was well advanced and the hard-working Cluster-folk believed in going to bed early. Keill knew that there was no security force, as such, within the Home – the main danger to security was Veynaan attack from the air – and the few folk who worked night shifts, tending the food tanks and other parts of the life support system, would be on the lower levels. And Keill was going upwards.

He walked quickly but boldly to the ascending walkway, and sped up the moving spiral. It ended, of course, at the main corridor that led to the meeting room, on the top level. But a quick search of intersecting passages located a ramp leading upwards, and a heavy door.

He eased the door open with infinite care, an eye pressed to the opening. Beyond, on the roof, he saw only blackness and a sky full of stars, heard only the moan of the bitter night wind.

Slipping out on to the roof, he paused in deep shadow, letting his eyes adjust. Soon the starlight showed him the bulky outlines of the laser cannon emplacements on the roof's edge, and the upthrust of the landing pad where one of the shuttle ships rested. He moved forward soundlessly. The pad was raised from the roof – at about his shoulder height. Ignoring the broad ramp that led up to the shuttle, he circled the pad, watching and listening. Only when he was satisfied that the shuttle was deserted did he slide up over the edge of the pad and move, a shadow among shadows, to the shuttle.

The loading bay was firmly closed, but the personnel airlock gave him no trouble. Inside the ship, the blackness balked even his night vision, but he moved by touch from the control room through the hatch leading to the broad area of the cargo hold. And there his exploring hand found switches that turned on dim illumination.

The hold was nearly empty, save for a metal container, like a solid block no larger than a cubic metre. Keill inspected it closely. There seemed to be no seams which indicated an opening, but there were two slight depressions on either side.

When he touched these, the top of the container slid aside.

Within, carefully gripped by contoured ceramic, lay a shiny metal ovoid. It was no more than half a metre long, and had fine filaments of circuitry and electronic hook-ups trailing from one end like the roots of a plant.

It looked like an innocent, commonplace piece of technology. But an instinctive certainty turned Keill colder than the bitter wind outside could ever do.

Shalet had hinted at some fearsome weapon. And Keill knew beyond doubt that he was looking at it.

But what was it? A bomb of some sort? Could an explosive device of that size be likely to 'finish off' the Veynaans, as Shalet had put it?

He reached a hand down gingerly, intending to turn the ovoid round and examine it more closely. But he did not complete the movement.

From outside, a sound had penetrated to his keen hearing. A muffled, metallic scrape.

Instantly Keill sent the container's heavy lid sliding back into place, switched off the illumination and moved without a sound into the control room, to crouch by the personnel airlock.

Footsteps sounded on the surface of the landing pad outside the ship.

Keill moved back into shadow. There was a chance that, if the unknown person entered, he might turn into the cargo

48

hold and allow Keill to slide out, unseen, through the airlock.

But in the event his luck extended even further. It was the shuttle's cargo bay that swung open, in the hold – and while it moved Keill took advantage of its sound to open the airlock, and slipped out of the ship just as the boots of the unknown visitor sounded within the hold.

Stealthily he crossed the hard, roughened surface of the landing pad and lowered himself over its edge into the deeper blackness of the roof beneath it.

And then his luck ran out.

With a faint humming the surface of the roof seemed to fall slowly away beneath his feet.

His reflexes urged him to leap upwards and away like a startled wild creature. But realization held him back.

The elevator.

He thought back to Shalet's guided tour. The elevator moved along a sizeable cylindrical vertical shaft, which would make the elevator a plain circular disc, auto-magnetically supported, and flush with the roof's surface when at the top of the shaft. So he had not noticed it in the darkness until he had stepped on to it and his weight had somehow triggered it.

The elevator slid smoothly downwards. But above, Keill heard the thud of hurrying boots. The mysterious visitor to the shuttle had not missed the hum of the mechanism.

A hand-torch flashed above, the light spilling down the smooth metal sides of the elevator shaft. Keill crouched, hugging the opposite side, while the light probed down. But the elevator had dropped farther, and the torch-beam seemed never quite to overtake it enough to pick out Keill's crouching form. He felt sure he had not been seen.

But there were no other openings into the elevator shaft. Keill rode it to the bottom, knowing that he was still in danger, if some night worker was waiting on the lowest level to see why the elevator was working.

When it came to rest at last, part of the cylinder wall – a

hatchway through which the elevator could be loaded – clicked open automatically. Dim light filtered through the opening, but nothing else. No sound, no shout of alarm.

He moved silently out of the shaft. The broad expanse of the loading area was cluttered with piled containers of ossidin. Here and there work-robots stood, inactive for the night, and banks of machinery and equipment rested equally silent in their pools of shadow.

There were no Clusterfolk visible, yet Keill took no chances, making full use of cover as he ghosted across the area. The corridor beyond was also empty as he sped to the walkway. But once on its upward spiral, he halted, hardly breathing. A sound from above – on the descending walkway, that twisted around the one he was on – so that he would be fully exposed to anyone coming down.

He sprang off the walkway on the next level, moving swiftly into the empty corridor. Pushing against the nearest doorway, he found it open, and peered through. Two rows of high, bulky tanks confronted him – the containers in which the basic nutrients that made up the Home's synthesized food were cultured.

Each tank's lip was higher than Keill's head, and they were packed close together, except for a wide passage down the centre of the chamber. Overhead, a system of narrow metal catwalks allowed supervisors to keep watch on the contents of the tanks.

Keill saw no one, though the chamber was well-lit. He heard nothing except the low gurglings and bubblings from the great tanks, and a background hum from the machinery that maintained conditions within each tank.

Silently he drifted forward along the central passage between the two rows of tanks, then halted. Faintly, from the far end of the chamber, he heard voices.

He moved further forward, crouching, listening. Two of the night supervisors, he judged, idly chatting at the end of one row of tanks. At any minute they might move towards him – along the passage, or along one of the overhead cat-walks.

He retraced his steps to the door where he had entered, and tugged at it gently. It did not move. He pulled more firmly. It remained solidly closed.

Somehow, while he had been in the chamber, it had been locked.

There would surely be another door out of the chamber. But that would mean going past the workmen at the far end. Perhaps, he thought, he could bluff his way past them, tell them he had lost his way.

He turned back towards the passage – and froze.

A work-robot was rolling in ominous near-silence along the passage, its scanner eye fixed on him, its six long metal arms stretching out threateningly towards him.

Keill stood still, studying the robot. It was a different design from the others he had seen. Its body was narrower and far taller, nearly three metres. And on the ends of the six tentacle arms were some different attachments, for use with the tanks – ladle-like scoops, flat paddle-like devices, but also two of the pincer-like grabs, resembling the claws of some weird crustacean.

It was almost upon him. And he knew there was no chance that it might just be going on its way harmlessly past him, in the course of its work. The eye was too firmly fixed on him. The arms were extending too obviously in his direction.

It was certainly being controlled. Which meant that some-one, on a nearby monitor screen, was watching him through the scanner. And guiding those arms.

Abruptly he took a step towards the robot and leaped – straight upwards. Catching the lip of the nearest tank, he swung lithely up on to its edge, and rose to his feet, gauging his next leap to the edge of the catwalk above.

He had moved with all his uncanny speed. But the lip of the tank was narrow, sloping and slippery – and whoever was controlling the robot was also dangerously quick.

In the fractional instant while he found his footing for the next leap, one of the tentacle arms – bearing a pincer grab – swept up at him. It moved like some metallic serpent, with gaping jaws, and the jaws struck at Keill's throat.

He swayed aside, evading the grab. As he did so, the other pincer-bearing tentacle struck. He parried that lunge with a forearm block.

But the metal arm twisted back on itself, and the powerful pincers clamped on to his wrist.

Effortlessly it jerked him up, off the tank's lip, dangling him by his wrist, helplessly, over the edge of the tank.

Below him the pungent, viscous fluid bubbled and heaved. For a moment he thought he was to be dropped into the thick sludge, which would be unpleasant but hardly fatal.

Then the robot's other arms were slashing and striking at him, the second grab again seeking his throat. As he dangled painfully from one wrist, he fought – swinging and spinning aside from the attacks, blocking or chopping at the twisting, serpentine arms.

Until, without warning, the arm that gripped his wrist swung him viciously downwards – intending to smash his body against the edge of the tank, as if he were a flapping fish on a line, to break his back with the impact.

He arched the muscles of his back just in time. Not his body but the soles of his boots took the force of the slamming impact against the tank. Every cell in his body seemed to be jarred out of place, but he had suffered no harm – save for the grinding pain from the relentless grip on his arm.

Again the robot lifted him and swung him violently down. Again Keill tried to blunt the impact with his feet. But the robot had slightly shifted its position. Keill's feet only plunged knee-deep into the thick, sticky nutrient. And, savagely, the robot's pincer smashed his right forearm against the lip of the tank.

The blow was intended to shatter the arm, so that Keill could no longer use its support to save himself from being beaten murderously against the tank.

But the arm did not break.

For a frozen moment the robot was motionless – as if its controller could not grasp what had happened, or what had not.

And Keill – despite the blazing, screaming pain from his bruised and torn right arm – did not miss his chance.

In that frozen instant, using his agonized wrist as a pivot, he flung his body backwards like a gymnast in a back roll over a horizontal bar. At the top of the backward curve, he straightened his legs, his body arrowing horizontally through the air.

Before the robot's controller could react, both boots smashed into the robot's scanner eye.

Shattered circuits spat sparks and smoke through the gaping hole in the plastiglass. The robot's controller, blinded now, threshed its arms wildly, furiously. But Keill had followed through the destruction of the eye by clamping his free hand on to the tentacle that gripped him. While it lashed and flailed, he rode it tenaciously – waiting his next chance.

It came soon. Each of the robot's arms sprouted out of a socket on the tall body that was guarded with a housing of plastic. Keill's eyes were fixed on that.

And when for a fractional second the arm he rode twisted and bent near to the body, he struck.

His boot flashed down with terrifying power, and a perfect aim. The heel drove irresistibly against the joint of arm and body.

And the metal arm sheared cleanly off.

Keill dropped to the floor, rolling swiftly away, still clutching what was now a limp length of flexible metal. The pincer-grip on his tormented wrist had opened, freeing him.

For a moment the blind robot still frantically struck and threshed around itself, twisting on its treads. But, when Keill easily evaded it, its arms dropped, its treads halted, and it was still.

Clearly its controller, lacking vision, had given up the attempt at murder.

Only then – crouched and wary, half-dazed with the pain in his right arm – did Keill hear the pounding feet in the passageway, the shouts of hurrying people.

Half the Clusterfolk seemed to have been aroused by the clamour, and to be crowding the corridors as the two pale and frightened workers took Keill to the Home's infirmary. He had rejected the idea of a stretcher and walked calmly through the throngs, paying them little attention, showing no exterior sign of the agony from his swollen, bleeding right arm.

The two workers, hurrying beside him, alternated between alarmed and puzzled apologies to Keill and explanations to the crowd. 'Can't understand it,' they were babbling. 'Don't have many robots go rogue. An' what you did – never saw the like. With a busted arm an' all.' And to the crowd, 'Robot went crazy. Nearly killed him. Sure, saw it all. Happened so quick – smashed it, he did. Bare-handed!'

And the crowd was still oohing and marvelling and staring avidly as Keill closed the infirmary door behind him.

He sat quiet and unmoving, while a sleepy medic fussed over his arm. Finally the medic stood back, shaking his head wonderingly.

'That's near miraculous,' he said. 'With these contusions and lacerations, and with what those supervisors are saying happened, you should have a severe compound fracture. You're very lucky.'

'As you say,' Keill nodded wearily. 'Lucky.'

'I've given you an injection,' the medic went on, 'that will reduce the pain and swelling, and I've put on a light synthaskin bandage. You should have full use of the arm in a day or two.'

As the medic turned away, Keill flexed the fingers of his right hand. The pain was distant, smothered, and already the forearm had returned to normal size thanks to the injection. No, he thought fiercely, I have full use of the arm *now*. And he made a mental note to send his thanks once again to the Overseers, for the unbreakable alloy that he bore within his body.

He turned as the door of the infirmary slammed open. Joss, her lovely face pale with concern, burst in with Shalet striding close behind her. As Keill stood up, Joss moved close to him, her eyes anxious as they moved from his face to his bandaged arm.

'You might have been killed!' she said.

Keill smiled, lifting his bandaged arm. 'I wasn't. Not even badly hurt.'

Joss looked startled. 'But everyone's saying that your arm was crushed!'

'Just cuts and bruises.' He waggled his fingers. 'The medic says it'll be fine in a day or two.'

'Takes more'n a rogue robot to beat a legionary, eh?' Shalet chortled.

Joss was frowning slightly. 'But what were you doing down there, anyway?'

That was the question Keill had been dreading. But there was no sign of strain in his voice or face as he replied. 'Couldn't sleep, so I was wandering,' he said easily. 'Anything to get out of that cubicle – it's worse than the escape capsule.'

Shalet's laughter boomed. 'Often feel that way m'self! What'd you do – forget which level y'were on?'

Keill nodded, putting on an embarrassed look. 'I must have miscounted, or got confused somehow.'

'Happens to strangers every time!' Shalet laughed. 'Joss, you better take him back to his cubicle, so he don't get lost again!'

Joss smiled. 'He won't. I'll see to that.'

Later, as sunrise was pushing wan grey light through the window-slit, Keill lay on his narrow bunk being scolded by a worried Glr.

I fail to see the value of being nearly caught, and nearly killed, just for a glimpse of a mysterious metal container, she was saying.

'No value at all,' Keill replied agreeably.

There was a pause. *I am glad you are unharmed,* Glr added, in a gentler tone.

Keill grinned. '*I am too.*'

And the arm will not affect you, regarding the 'task' that Quern mentioned?

'No. It's not badly hurt – and I heal quickly.'

Good, Glr said. *The Overseers are extremely anxious to learn the nature of the weapon. Your 'task' may expose some of Quern's secrets.*

'I've already learned one thing,' Keill said darkly. 'Someone on the Cluster doesn't want me alive. That robot was controlled, no question of it. My guess would be by Fillon – or Groll, if he can handle robots.'

Whoever it was, Glr replied, *he was no doubt acting on Quern's orders. So we cannot discount a sinister possibility.* She paused for a moment, then went on sombrely: *There may well be a second Deathwing agent on the Cluster.*

chapter six

Keill spent most of the next day resting in his cubicle, to speed the healing of his injury, and also to avoid more awed curiosity from the Clusterfolk, who would all have heard of the robot's attack. Joss visited him briefly at midday, bringing a meal that they shared – but she seemed slightly nervous, preoccupied with her own thoughts, and Keill commented on it.

She smiled wanly. 'Sorry. There's a great deal to do. Everything seems to be coming to a head so quickly.'

Interest sparked in Keill, but he kept his voice light. 'You seem to have a lot of responsibility.'

She nodded. 'Quern relies on me to coordinate everything when he's not here. I seem to spend all my time at it.'

'Don't the other Councillors help?'

'When they can. But all of them have their Cluster jobs as well.'

'And you don't?'

'Not really. I've had a lot of jobs on the Cluster, but just before we broke with Veynaa I was mostly piloting the ultra-freighter. And of course it's not in use now.'

'Nice job,' Keill said, trying to sound casual. 'What do the other Councillors do?'

'They're all fairly specialized. Shalet supervises a clerical section, Bennen and Rint are technicians in the ventilation and cleaning works. Fillon's more special – he's probably the best computer person in the Home.'

Keill's face was blank, but within he was grimly exultant. Every aspect of the Home's technology involved computers – including the robots.

'Maybe he ought to have a look at that robot,' Keill said calmly. 'To see what went wrong.'

'That's been done,' she said. 'Maintenance took it apart this morning. But the damage you caused made it hard for them to spot any earlier malfunction.'

He nodded, pretending indifference. 'On the subject of jobs, what does my friend Groll do? Just hit people?'

'No,' she smiled, 'he's a manual worker in the loading bay. Why?'

'No reason.' Not Groll, then, he thought – but very possibly Fillon. 'Just so I know where to avoid. I don't think he likes my company.'

Joss shook her head, laughing. 'Not even Groll would look for trouble with a man who can wreck a robot bare-handed.' She glanced down at his arm. 'How are the after-effects?'

'It aches a little,' Keill said, flexing his fingers, 'but it does what I tell it to.'

'Good. Because Quern's due back this evening – and I think he'll want to get things started right away.'

Those words, after she left, began an anticipation within Keill that grew throughout the afternoon – and rose even higher when, near sunset, he received no response to an attempt to reach Glr.

So Quern was on his way, within his own mental range of the Cluster, and Glr had set up the shielding again in her own and Keill's minds.

His anticipation reached a new peak soon afterwards when Joss returned to Keill's cubicle. No longer preoccupied, she showed the same barely contained excitement Keill had seen before. She glowed and sparkled, and Keill could hardly take his eyes off her as they went towards the meeting room, where, she said, Quern was waiting.

The albino sat as before at the long table, with the full Council in attendance. To Keill's surprise, Groll was there as well, lounging sullenly against the far wall.

'I'm told we nearly lost you,' Quern said, without a trace of concern in his cold voice.

'Nearly,' Keill said. Then, on impulse, he added: 'For a moment I felt the wing of death upon me.'

He had no doubt that a flicker of response showed in the red-rimmed, deep-set eyes. Surprise, perhaps, or wariness – but also, oddly, a trace of sardonic amusement.

'Most poetic,' Quern murmured. 'And is it true that you have not been . . . put out of action?'

Keill lifted his lightly bandaged arm. 'It's healing.'

'How fortunate. And, from what I hear of the occurrence, how extremely . . . astonishing, that your injury should be so minor.' He studied Keill coldly for a moment. 'You are a very unusual man, in many ways.'

Keill felt certain that Quern was alluding partly to the mind-shield, which would be a mystery still to the albino. And he was also certain, though he felt nothing, that at that moment Glr would be resisting another of Quern's battering probes at Keill's mind.

To distract him, Keill said curtly, 'I doubt if you brought me here to inquire after my health.'

'No, indeed.' Quern leaned back, folding his bony hands. 'Our preparations are now complete and before another day has passed we will have brought the planet Veynaa to its knees. Only the final steps in my . . . in *our* plan remain to be taken.'

Keill waited, saying nothing.

'Tonight,' the chill voice went on, 'a raiding party from the Cluster will visit one of the communication satellites above Veynaa. The party will intrude a tape into the planetary vid system, which will issue our ultimatum to the Veynaan authorities.'

Keill raised an eyebrow. 'And the whole planet will simply lie down and surrender?'

'Precisely.' Quern's smile was icy. 'Because the vid tape will also inform the Veynaans what will happen if they do not.'

'Are you going to let me in on the secret?' Keill asked.

'I think you have an inkling of it already,' Quern said, glancing coldly at Shalet. 'Hints have been dropped that you will not have missed – about the weapon that I have provided for the Cluster.'

Keill waited, his face a mask.

'The weapon is extremely powerful, and quite irresistible,' Quern continued. 'Were it used, it could . . . damage much of the planet.'

Keill stared coldly round the table at the Councillors. 'You would consider using such a thing? Shalet? Joss?'

Neither replied. Shalet gnawed her lower lip unhappily, looking down at the table, but Joss met his gaze firmly, her face pale and determined. Quern raised a long hand.

'It will not need to be used. I have arranged a . . . demonstration of the weapon's effect, on one of the dead outer planets of this system. That will be enough to convince the Veynaans.'

'What if it isn't?' Keill asked angrily, aware of a subtly false tone in Quern's voice. 'What if the Veynaans refuse to give way? Will you use the weapon then?'

'They will *not* refuse,' Quern snapped. 'Veynaans are realists, not romantic fools. They will see that they have no choice.'

Again Keill's gaze swept the table, but there was to be no help there. Joss's eyes were hard and bright with the zeal of a revolutionary; Fillon was smiling with smug delight. Shalet and the two old men looked nervous, but Quern's influence seemed to have overwhelmed them.

Keill controlled his anger. Quern and his deadly plan would have to be stopped – but not here, he knew. And not with words. 'And what's my role in all this?' he asked curtly. 'This task you mentioned?'

'Your task is the one most suitable for a legionary,' Quern said, the icy smile returning. 'You are to lead the raid on the Veynaan satellite.'

The plan, as Quern unfolded it, was devastatingly simple. A group of five would take a shuttle up to the ultrafreighter. They would then transfer the mysterious weapon to the freighter and would pilot it away from the Cluster and into a parking orbit around Veynaa.

Three of them would then take the shuttle for the raid on the communications satellite, while the remaining two completed adjustments to the weapon.

The three raiders would then pick up the other two from the freighter and return to the Cluster. And the freighter would remain, orbiting Veynaa with its cargo of death.

Keill could see problems and flaws, but he left them unspoken. 'Who else is coming?' he asked, when the albino had finished.

'Myself, of course,' Quern smiled, 'in charge of the weapon. Our lovely Joss will pilot the freighter, and will stay on it to lend me her . . . delicate skills. Fillon will go with you, and will insert the tape into the vid system. And Groll, here, will accompany you as well – to ensure that you do not forget where your . . . loyalties lie.'

'If you still distrust me, Quern,' Keill said flatly, 'why tell me all this? Why include me at all?'

Quern leaned forward, all humour banished from the death-white face. 'Because your skills will be useful, and because it is the best way to keep an eye on you, Randor. Nor is there any harm in telling you the plan – because it will go forward this very night, and the five of us will remain together every second from now till we enter the shuttle.'

The red-rimmed eyes glittered. 'One more thing, Randor,' Quern went on. 'You will not be armed during the raid, but Groll will be. Should you show the slightest sign of interfering with the plan, Groll has been instructed to kill you without hesitation.'

*

Keill leaned forward from the narrow acceleration seat to peer past Quern through the shuttle's viewpoint. Ahead, the ultrafreighter loomed, a vast silhouette against the stars, dwarfing the shuttle.

Quern, at the shuttle's controls, glanced back. 'Growing impatient, Randor?' he sneered.

Keill ignored the question. 'You realize that the moment Fillon puts that tape into the vid system, the Veynaans will throw ships up at the satellite.'

'No doubt. But they will not at first know *which* of their satellites has been attacked. By the time they do, you will have made your escape and be out of range.'

'Even so, they'll look for us,' Keill persisted. 'And they're likely to spot the freighter. What's to stop them blasting it to atoms?'

'Two things,' Quern replied with a frozen smile. 'The tape will have told them that the weapon will activate if tampered with. And to be doubly sure, I will have specially programmed the freighter. It will move in and out of Overlight at random points on its orbit – so the Veynaans will never pinpoint where it is, or where it will be.'

Keill sat back, considering. The freighter was not equipped with the standard ion-energy drive for short-run planetary travel – it had only minimal boosters, to keep its orbit constant around a planet when it was stationary. But it was equipped with the Overlight drive, for interstellar flight. So it could move cargo across the galaxy as quickly as a ship with planetary drive could cross a solar system.

Keill grudgingly realized that Quern had covered most possibilities, that the plan had every chance of succeeding. But if the Veynaans bowed to the threat, and gave way to the Cluster's demands, Keill also knew that the Cluster would merely find itself in the grip of new, far more deadly rulers. And the Warlord would have control of the priceless supply of ossidin.

No, he told himself fiercely, there will be a time – some-where along the stages of the plan – when Quern can be stopped. And will be.

The shuttle was nosing up now to the huge sweep of the freighter's hull. A docking bay opened automatically, like a vast maw, at the stern of the giant ship, and the shuttle drifted in, retros throbbing, to settle on a landing pad. The bay closed, sealing itself against the vacuum of space, and the shuttle's drive faded into silence.

They waited in that silence for several moments. Again Keill peered out, studying the shadowy interior of the freighter. It was little more than an enormous shell, he knew, with solid bulkheads extending its full height and breadth to divide it into several separate compartments.

He also knew that such freighters had basic life-support systems and minimal gravity, not only in their control rooms but throughout the whole of the great shell, to maintain the condition of cargo. They were waiting now for atmosphere and pressure to be restored after the docking bay had closed.

Shortly Quern and Joss rose and moved towards the air-lock of the shuttle. Quern looked down at Keill. 'You three will remain here – and try not to let your curiosity get the better of you, Randor. When I signal, your work begins.'

Keill did not reply, but merely slid forward into the pilot's seat. Behind him Groll stirred, and Keill glanced briefly back. The big man sat glowering, once again cradling a laserifle, while next to him Fillon stared worriedly after Quern.

All three were spacesuited, in readiness for their attack on the satellite. And Keill was glad that he had been able to collect his own spacesuit before leaving the Cluster. Legion spacesuits were specially made, unusually light and flexible so they would not hamper a legionary's movements. Keill had no doubt that, unarmed in Groll's company, there might come a time when he would need to move with all his speed.

He turned back and looked again through the viewport.

The great shell of the freighter was deserted – though in the gloomy depths next to the wall of the nearest bulkhead he could see the forms of some work-robots, motionless, inactive.

He could also see, stretching out from the landing pad, the metallic shine of two parallel auto-magnetic strips, on a trackway that presumably ran all the way to the control room in the freighter's distant nose. The trackway was fixed high along the side of the freighter, many metres above the deck of the hold where the robots stood. Along the strips ran low, wheel-less, two-seater vehicles that carried personnel back and forth within the freighter.

And as Keill watched, Quern and Joss came into view, riding one of the personnel carriers as they moved away from the shuttle.

Keill's eyes shifted downwards, to a work-robot, rolling along in the gloom of the deck below, bearing the metal container he had seen before on the shuttle.

Both carrier and robot vanished through openings in the great bulkhead. Several silent minutes later, Keill felt an eerie sensation deep within his body, as if at the nucleus of each cell. But he hardly noticed it, for it was long familiar to him. It meant that the freighter had entered Overlight.

There was no sense of movement within Overlight. It was not so much travel as transference. When that unique field came into being round a ship, the ship no longer existed in any real sense. It had left the known universe, where the laws of nature held true, and had begun something like a shortcut through a realm where no one knew for certain what sort of laws operated, if any. In Overlight a ship was in nothingness, in a non-place, beyond human imagining.

Keill knew that, had they been able to see outside the freighter just then, the viewscreens would have revealed only a void, a total, empty formlessness without colour, texture or depth. By comparison, even the blank vacuum of deep space at the rim of the galaxy seemed lively and welcoming.

Because the freighter was moving only from one planet to another within the same system, the almost unfelt physical sensation occurred again within only a few seconds. So the freighter had arrived in an orbit around Veynaa, and had returned to normal space. It would have to be well beyond the planet, Keill knew. Ships did not risk entering or leaving Overlight when they were within a planet's gravitational pull. It did strange things to the Overlight field, and no one took risks with Overlight.

Quern's cold voice sounded from the communicator.

'You will lift off now.' The voice grew even colder. 'And remember, Randor – no mistakes, or you die.'

chapter seven

Keill swept the shuttle along the course that its computer, pre-set by Quern, had worked out, towards the Veynaan communication satellite. Within a few minutes the freighter's bulk had vanished into the glimmering black depths behind them. Many long minutes later, the pinpoint of light that was the satellite winked into view ahead.

The retros boomed into action, and Keill delicately jockeyed the shuttle, swinging it close to the satellite, reducing speed, until at last it came to what seemed like rest in a perfect parking orbit less than thirty metres from their goal.

All three wordlessly checked their suits and fastened their helmets. Keill noticed beads of sweat on Fillon's forehead and recognized the groundsman's terror of leaving a ship in vacuum. But there was no risk. They would move across the intervening space with flitters – small, hand-held cylinders that released bursts of compressed gas, enough to propel them ahead and to control their free-fall movements.

Only when they reached the satellite would an element of risk occur. But Quern had assured them that such satellites contained at most a maintenance and control staff of two men, only one of whom was on duty at a time. And the shuttle's arrival would not have alerted them: Keill had brought it in from the rear, out of sight from the satellite's viewports, while the noise of their arrival could not, of course, travel in vacuum.

He reached to the sleeve pocket of his suit and took out the flitter cylinder. Opening the airlock, he jerked his head at the other two, and stepped out into space. He sailed ahead slowly, staring at the immense wheeling curve of the planet Veynaa, dominating his range of vision, the thin cloud cover in its atmosphere drawn like veils across clearly visible land masses.

Then he let his body curve slightly to glance back. Fillon had clearly been reluctant, for Groll had a tight grip on one of his arms as if he had had to drag the other man out. They, too, curved in free-fall, the laserifle swinging slowly where it was slung across Groll's shoulders, until a burst of ice crystals showed that Groll had fired his flitter, to bring their glide on target.

Keill fired his own flitter, and the three figures surged silently towards the satellite.

It was more precisely a space station, resembling two slightly flattened eggs joined at their sides and bristling with aerials, solar panels and a complicated tangle of other equipment. Keill had no difficulty in opening the outer door of its airlock, and then they were standing in the chamber of the lock, already feeling the artificial gravity grip them, waiting for the inner door to open.

If something had gone wrong, Keill knew, they might well find themselves staring at the muzzle of a gun. He gathered himself on a fine edge of readiness.

But it seemed that the Veynaan who was on duty had been dulled by tedium and sleepiness. The inner door was halfway open before his frozen, horrified stare at the men in the airlock changed into a scrambling lunge for a hand-gun, resting on a nearby panel.

By then Keill had almost reached him. But in the last second, Groll's laserbeam scorched past Keill's shoulder and drilled a small, neat hole in the Veynaan's head. The man collapsed face forward on to the panel, a thread of smoke rising from the singed hair.

Keill whirled in fury. 'You didn't need to kill him!' he shouted into his helmet communicator.

'Ain't takin' chances,' Groll snarled, his finger still curled over the firing stud.

'Try to fire that thing again,' Keill told him coldly, 'and I'll take it away from you and stuff it down your throat.'

His eyes locked with Groll's, and for a moment the big man seemed about to take the challenge. But then Groll's eyes shifted, and his finger slid away from the stud.

Keill turned away, in time to see the hatchway connecting the two segments of the satellite swing open. Through it stumbled the second Veynaan, half-asleep, yawning and rubbing his eyes.

He had no time even to open those eyes before Keill sprang. Nor did Groll have time to swing his rifle round. The knuckle of Keill's middle finger struck a perfectly weighted blow just behind the Veynaan's ear. He sighed and crumpled, and Keill eased him to the floor.

'You sure keen on keepin' Veynaans alive,' Groll rumbled.

Keill ignored him. 'Fillon – get moving!' he barked.

Fillon, who had been watching tremulously, jumped and scuttled quickly over to the panel where the dead Veynaan had been sitting. For Keill, even with his fair grounding in computer and communication systems, the tangle of equipment was a maze that would have taken weeks to sort through. But Fillon's hands moved unerringly among the circuits, making the cross-connections that would allow the inserted tape to override the system.

As he watched, Keill toyed with the idea of disarming Groll and preventing the tape from being broadcast. But in the end he rejected it. Quern would certainly be alerted by such an action – and stopping the Cluster's taped ultimatum was far less important than stopping Quern.

He stepped towards the hatch into the other section. Quern had said there were only two men on the satellite, but no professional fighting man would take another's word on such a matter – even less Quern's. Silently he entered the compartment, his eyes sweeping over the unmade bunks, the discarded clothing, the clutter and mess created by two bored men living together in a tiny capsule in space. But only two.

Satisfied, Keill turned back towards the hatch. It had swung shut behind him. But when he grasped the handle and twisted it, the hatch did not budge.

It was locked, or jammed. And Keill knew beyond doubt that it was no accident.

'Groll!' he shouted.

No reply. His helmet communicator remained silent.

'Don't be stupid, Groll! Open it!'

Silence.

Keill took a step backwards, and another. He neither knew nor cared, just then, what Groll was trying to do, whether he was carrying out Quern's orders or acting on his own. Within Keill at that moment there was no room for analytic thought. There was merely a controlled but towering anger.

He breathed deeply, gathering that anger, channelling it, letting it flow and mix with the adrenalin that was pouring power through his body. Then he exploded into movement, leaping at the hatch.

At the instant that a sharp yell burst from his lips, focusing the release of power, his booted foot smashed with terrifying force just above the hatchway's handle.

The hatch was made of the same metal as the satellite's hull, as the hull of most spacecraft. True, the hatch contained only one layer – but it was the strongest, most resistant metal that technological man had yet devised.

But the metal bulged like a blister beneath the impact of Keill's boot. And the hatch flew open as if on springs, slamming back resoundingly against the wall on the far side.

Keill leaped through the opening. The dead Veynaan had slid to the floor, the unconscious one lay where Keill had left him. Otherwise the compartment was empty.

He hurtled to the airlock, willing it to more speed as the inner door opened, closed, and the outer door slid aside.

Snatching the flitter from his sleeve pocket, Keill stepped

out into space – in time to see the shuttle just beginning to edge away from its parking orbit. Helpless, he ground his teeth in rage as he watched the bulbous ship curve away, accelerating, the flame of its drive dwindling into a light-speck as it sped away into the distance.

Then from another part of the limitlessness around him, Keill's eye caught sight of other points of light.

Spacecraft – five at least – hurtling up from the surface of the planet, clearly on a course that would bring them to the satellite.

Keill drifted for a moment, just beyond the airlock, knowing that the Veynaans were still too far away to see him, a comparatively minute speck in the vastness. As he watched, the five ships changed course. Their detectors had clearly picked up the fleeing shuttle, and they swept away in pursuit.

They would be very unlikely to catch it, he thought, before it could reach the freighter. And the freighter would simply go into Overlight, to reappear on the other side of the planet, beyond the reach of the pursuers.

Then, of course, the Veynaans would turn back to the satellite.

More calmly, he weighed his chances.

He could use the flitter to get out into space, far enough away to be undetectable by the ships when they returned. But that would exhaust the flitter and he would be stranded – and a call to Glr would be his only hope.

But he could not reach Glr until Quern returned to the Cluster. Only then would she know that Keill, whose mind she would still be shielding, had been left behind in space.

Then, of course, she would come at once, being able to drop the shields when she and Keill were both out of Quern's telepathic range. But it would all depend on Quern moving back to the Cluster quickly – before the airpack on Keill's spacesuit became exhausted.

Otherwise . . .

He grimaced, disliking the idea of floating helplessly in space and merely hoping that Quern would move in time. No, far better to stay on the satellite, Veynaans or not.

After all, they would not expect to find anyone there but their own men. He would have the element of surprise, at first, and he would have the gun of the dead Veynaan inside if he needed it. The ships would not blast the satellite itself, not with a Veynaan alive inside as a hostage. At least, he hoped they wouldn't.

In any case, he thought fiercely, I'd rather make a fight of it here, whatever happens, than drift around out there and suffocate.

The flitter fired, and he dived back into the satellite's airlock.

Back inside, he unfastened his helmet and placed it within reach, then picked up the dead Veynaan's gun – an energy gun, he saw gratefully – and tucked it into a leg pocket on his suit.

The other Veynaan was beginning to stir and moan. Keill bent and lifted him effortlessly, carrying him into the other compartment and dumping him on a bunk, then tying his hands with the sleeves of a dirty shirt plucked from the floor.

Returning to the main compartment, he glanced round, establishing the layout in his mind. The communication equipment almost encircled him, in banks and cabinets against the hull of the satellite, leaving a sizeable clear area directly in front of the airlock. He would be better off in the other compartment, he thought, when the Veynaans arrived.

But before he could move, his attention was caught by the picture on the broad display of monitor screens, above the place where the dead Veynaan had sat. A large, florid man was pictured on all the screens – a man wearing a lavishly decorated uniform of some sort, and a ferociously angry expression.

Curious, Keill moved closer to watch and listen.

'... have heard the demands and threats of the Cluster rebels,' the uniformed Veynaan was saying. 'The people of Veynaa will not need me to tell them that these demands are outrageous. In fact, they are insane.' His voice grated. 'That is what has overtaken the leaders of the rebellion – insanity, and evil.'

If you knew how right you were, Keill thought, watching.

'You will also have heard the ultimatum from the rebels,' the man on the screen went on, 'which gives us twenty-four hours to submit to their terms. Submit!' The man spat the word as if it were poison. 'But the government and military authorities have authorized me to tell you this: we will not submit. Veynaa will not give away its most priceless asset – it will not bow down to madmen and murderers.'

Quern had said the Veynaans were hard-headed realists, Keill remembered. Hard-headed they certainly seemed to be.

The man on the screen was growing more furious with every word. 'All Veynaans will also have heard the rebels' threat – to attack our world if we do not accept their terms. Most of you will have felt that threat to be absurd, impossible. But I must tell you that it is a serious threat – and the authorities are taking it seriously.' His voice darkened. 'The rebels have acquired some sort of destructive device – and they demonstrated its power, for us, on the dead outer planet of this system, Xentain. But they did not know – or did not care, if they knew – that our exploratory team had landed on Xentain some weeks ago. That there were two hundred and thirty Veynaans on Xentain when the rebels launched their ... demonstration. Today the planet is as dead as it ever was, and all of them with it.'

The man's voice was ragged with pain as well as rage. And Keill too felt chilled by the revelation, by the pointless, unnecessary killing. He knew that the speaker was right – that Quern would not have cared, if he had known, about the exploratory team.

'We sent a robot ship to relay back pictures of Xentain as it now is,' the man went on. His image began to fade, and another image to replace it.

And though the Veynaan's voice went on speaking, Keill heard no more words. He was staring rigidly at the screen, pale with shock, clenched fists white-knuckled, his mind a swirling tumult of horror.

It was a sight he had seen once before in reality, and a thousand times since in nightmare.

A planet surrounded by a glowing, pulsating, golden nimbus of lethal radiation.

Just as his world, Moros, had been, on that terrible day when the Legions had died.

Through the waves of horror and shock, Keill fought for control, and found it, as, deeper within him, a steel-cold, hate-filled, relentless rage began to form and build. Final proof was there on the screen, if it had been needed, that Quern was of the Deathwing, an agent of the Warlord, and that he was threatening to do to Veynaa what had been done to Moros.

The ghastly image of glowing death vanished from the screen, and the uniformed Veynaan returned. 'Our scientists say that this is a totally new form of radiation. They cannot say what it is, or how it is formed – only that it is lethal, and long-lasting.' His fist slammed fiercely on to the table before him. 'But we will not panic – and we will not *submit*! We will meet this monstrosity with our anger – our courage – our strength!'

The speaker also now struggled for control, rubbing a hand across his face. 'Your local governors have begun preparations. Protective clothing will be issued, shelters will be prepared, as far as possible in the time we have. Key personnel from each district will be evacuated offplanet, as many as the available spacecraft can take. But these, people of Veynaa, are merely precautions. Your government is convinced, without any doubt, that the rebels' threat is a *bluff* — that not even they would dare to use such a weapon against a planet of six million people!'

Fool, thought Keill coldly. You don't know who you're fighting — or what.

'In any case,' the Veynaan went on grimly, 'they will not get a chance to do so. They will be stopped — and our dead, on Xentain, will be avenged. Plans are now well advanced for a *full military strike* against the Cluster. We will wipe those vermin off the face of their planet, and reduce their nest to rubble!'

'You can't!' Keill heard himself shout. Fools twice over, he thought — for the moment that attack is launched, Quern will activate the weapon, and every living thing on Veynaa will die!

His mind raced. He could hardly set out to stop the Veynaans and their blindly vengeful plans. Which meant that he would have to stop Quern — and somehow also warn the Cluster.

And that meant returning to the Cluster — back into Quern's grip.

As his mind feverishly began to make plans, the inner door of the airlock hissed open behind him.

chapter eight

Keill spun, reaching for the gun in his pocket, but as instantly letting his hand drop. The two spacesuited men in the airlock were both armed – and their surprise at seeing him had not prevented them from levelling their energy guns at him.

They stepped in warily, glancing round, their guns unwavering as they unfastened the visors of their space helmets and raised them. Their faces were brown, leathery, seamed – the faces of experienced spacemen, veteran regulars in the Veynaan armed forces.

'Lookit this,' the taller of the two said. 'They left one behind.'

Keill neither moved nor spoke.

'I'll take a look around,' the shorter one said. 'Watch him.'

The short man moved to one side, professionally cautious, staying well out of Keill's reach. 'Should be two technicians,' he growled. 'What've you . . .'

He stopped, catching sight of the body of the dead Veynaan. His eyes narrowed and his brown face flushed with rage as he saw the entry wound, the darkened stream of blood on the dead man's hair. 'They killed one!'

The taller Veynaan, glaring, raised his gun to sight carefully at Keill's face. 'Make it one for one.'

'Wait,' said the short man – a fractional instant before Keill moved.

The gun was lowered, and Keill held back, still standing relaxed and silent.

'Somebody's gonna want to talk to this one,' the short one explained.

'Yeh.' The tall one looked disappointed. 'Have a look in the other part. And call the other ships, tell 'em what we found.'

As the shorter one moved to the hatch of the other compartment, Keill was savouring the meaning of his words. The other ships of the squad he had seen were elsewhere – probably still seeking the shuttle. These two Veynaans had come alone to the satellite.

'Hey!' The shorter one was staring at the bulging dent in the hatch, the shattered lock. 'What could've done this?'

The surprise in his voice made the taller man involuntarily begin to turn his head. Before he realized his mistake, Keill had dived.

It was a headlong, flat, low tackle that swept the Veynaan's legs from under him while his gun flared harmlessly above Keill's head. The tall man sprawled on top of Keill in a tangle of threshing arms and legs, until Keill slammed an elbow into his belly and drove all breath and fight out of him.

The shorter man was cursing and bobbing back and forth, trying to get a clear shot that would not endanger his friend. But Keill's own gun seemed to leap into his hand, and its energy beam bit into the Veynaan's upper arm.

He shrieked and dropped his gun, staggering backwards, clutching his seared arm, and overbalanced as he stumbled through the hatchway. Then Keill was on his feet, snatching up his helmet and leaping for the airlock.

By the time the outer door had opened his helmet was fastened and the flitter was in his hand. Beyond, a slender, needle-nosed Veynaan fighter floated silently, keeping pace with the satellite. Keill hurled himself into space towards it.

As he did so, the inner voice of Glr clamoured into his mind.

Keill! What in the cosmos are you doing out there?

'*At the moment,*' Keill said laconically, '*stealing a Veynaan fighter. What are you doing?*'

Coming to find you, Glr replied. *The sensors told me that Quern and the shuttle have returned to the Cluster. Yet I knew that your mind – which I was still shielding – was in space near Veynaa. What happened?*

'Tell you later,' Keill said quickly. In the distance he had caught sight of five tell-tale points of light, moving in his direction. *In a minute I'll have five other fighters on my tail. Keep coming.*

I am ready to enter Overlight now, Glr said.

'Will you be able to locate me?'

Keill, I could pinpoint your mind from across the galaxy, Glr said calmly.

Her mind withdrew as Keill plunged through the airlock of the Veynaan ship and into its narrow, tunnel-like interior, flinging himself into one of the two contoured seats at the control panel. It was a compact, up-to-date ship, much like fighters that Keill had often flown with the Legions. Rather have my own, he thought, but it'll do.

As he fed power to the drive, veering the ship away from the satellite, the viewscreens showed a spacesuited figure framed in the satellite's airlock. A gun in the figure's hand spat an energy beam, but it crackled harmlessly past as Keill swung the ship up and out of range.

But the other five Veynaan ships had sighted him, no doubt being told by the men in the satellite what had happened to their ship. They were closing fast, in battle formation.

Without hesitation, Keill sent his ship leaping ahead, its drive bellowing like a challenge – straight at the centre of the formation.

The manoeuvre clearly took the others by surprise. The formation wobbled a bit, then tightened as Keill flashed towards them.

They've recovered well, Keill thought to himself. They'll be ready to fire just about . . .

Now.

Hands flashing over the controls, Keill cut power and brutally forced the nose of the ship down. It fell away, twisting and fishtailing – as five energy beams blazed through the space it had vacated.

At once Keill slammed on full power and jerked the ship up again, its drive howling, its own beam raking upwards.

Bright flame exploded from the sterns of the two ships in the middle of the attacking group. As they faltered, Keill flashed between them, neatly intersecting the path of the attackers.

The two damaged ships spiralled away. Keill ignored them, knowing that they were only disabled, and should reach the planet safely if the pilots were good enough. He dragged the ship over in a tight loop, his eyes blurring darkly for a moment as the gravs clutched him, the ship shuddering and vibrating in protest. The three remaining Veynaans had also begun to wheel, in a gentler curve, but then frantically tried to twist round to bring their guns to bear as they found Keill sweeping down on top of them.

Before they could find their aim, Keill's gun fired again, slashing into the body of one of the ships – which whirled crazily away, out of control.

In the same moment, thundering out of the emptiness, Glr was there, the forward guns of Keill's fighter ablaze.

One of the two remaining Veynaan ships jerked upwards as if it had run into an invisible wall. Keill felt rather than heard the explosion as flame gushed from a gaping rent in its hull.

And the fifth and last ship lost no time in changing course, fleeing at top speed into the distance.

We missed one, Glr's voice said.

'*We must be out of practice*,' Keill replied with a grin.

Glr's laughter bubbled as she swung Keill's ship near. Keill thought he had never seen anything so welcome as that sleek, blunt-nosed, wedge shape, its blue Legion circlet gleaming.

He set the Veynaan ship's computer, to leave it drifting, and once again leaped out into space, to float across into the opening airlock of his own ship.

As he stepped into his ship's interior, Glr rose to greet him – whirling around the cramped space in one wild, delighted circuit, the tips of her wide, diaphanous wings clattering against the bulkheads. Then she settled abruptly on to his shoulder, her little hands gripping him with painful strength, making Keill glad that she had remembered to keep her talons retracted.

He craned round to look at her, grinning, and her round eyes glowed at him like small moons. He reached up to run an affectionate hand over the overlapping plates of skin like soft leather that covered her domed head and small, compact body – then snatched his hand away as she playfully snapped at him, a glint of sharp little fangs within her short muzzle.

I suppose I should be glad to see you, her mental voice said, striving for a grumbling tone. *But I am not happy at being caged in this ship for so long. I have nearly forgotten what it is like to spread my wings fully.*

Keill moved towards the controls. *'When this is over,'* he promised, *'I'll take you somewhere that is the most perfect place for flying in the galaxy.'*

How would you know, ground-crawler? she replied, her laughter rising.

As Keill slid into the familiar supporting grip of his sling-seat, Glr hopped from his shoulder to her own place, which Keill had rigged for her, above the control panel. It supported her small body, and also had attachments to which she could fasten the finger-hooks on the upper joints of her membranous wings, leaving her hands – which were also her feet – free to handle the controls. Not so much a sling-seat, Keill had said when he had finished it, as a sling-perch.

Settled, she turned her bright round eyes to Keill again, her silent merriment fading to seriousness. *Now,* she said, *tell me.*

Quickly Keill related everything that had happened from the moment that he had left the Cluster on the shuttle with

Quern and the others, up to the nature of the monstrous weapon now orbiting Veynaa, and also what he had learned from the satellite's monitor screens.

Glr was gravely silent for a moment. *Do you think*, she asked at last, *the Veynaan humans will be foolish enough to risk attacking the Cluster?*

'Not much doubt of it,' Keill said. 'They're angry, and they're looking for revenge. People do foolish things when they feel like that.'

Humans do foolish things much of the time, Glr replied primly. *For example, you are doubtless now going to return to the Cluster, although Quern will surely have you killed on sight.*

'He can try,' Keill said. 'But he has to be stopped – and I can't do that sitting out here.'

Very well. There was a troubled note in Glr's silent voice. *Will you land your ship openly?*

'I'll have to. But I'll put it down somewhere safely out of sight of the Home, and those cannon.'

Then he realized what was troubling Glr. 'I'm sorry,' he added gently. 'I don't like taking you back into Quern's range.'

No matter, Glr sighed. *He was probing your shield constantly, when you were near him – it is a relief to be away from that power. But the shields will withstand him, for as long as is necessary. And it will be useful if I am near to hand with the ship, in case you need help.*

Keill nodded, reaching for the controls. But Glr stopped him.

Before you enter Overlight, give me time to report to the Overseers. They will be growing anxious.

'Fine. I'll get myself some food while you do so – I don't expect much hospitality on the Cluster.'

The Overseers will want to know what you intend to do, Glr added.

'Tell them I'm going to get into the Home, one way or another, and warn the Clusterfolk – against Quern as much as against the Veynaans.'

And if the Clusterfolk will not listen?

'Then – whoever tries to stop me – I'll have to kill Quern.'

part three

To save a world

chapter nine

Emerging from Overlight, Keill sent his ship arrowing down towards the misshapen collection of planetoids and asteroids that was the Cluster. Glr stirred, her inner voice sounding strained.

Keill, the Overseers are deeply concerned. They think that the aggressive reaction of Veynaa was foreseen by the Warlord, and was a part of his plan all along. One way or another, Quern will seek to destroy the planet, to give the Warlord total control over the Cluster. And the Overseers fear that the memory of Moros, and its similar destruction, will make you reckless.

Keill grinned tightly. 'Let Quern worry about that.'

But Glr did not reply, for then they were nearing atmosphere, at the threshold of Quern's telepathic reach.

On the control panel the communicator crackled into life.

'This is Clusterhome. Identify yourself.'

'Keill Randor,' he snapped. 'I'm coming in.'

A gasp of surprise from the voice at the other end. 'Randor! They said you were dead!'

'They were wrong. Let me speak to Joss, or Shalet.'

'They're all in the meetin' room, next level,' said the Clusterman. 'I'll get 'em.'

A pause, while the image of the Cluster on the viewscreens seemed to be rushing towards the ship, ever larger.

Then Joss's voice, breathless with astonishment. 'Keill! Groll said you'd been killed!'

'Groll's wishful thinking,' Keill said. 'Is Quern with you?'

'The Council is in the meeting room,' she replied. 'Quern too – finalizing plans for when the Veynaans reply to the ultimatum.'

'They'll reply all right.' Quickly he outlined what he had heard on the satellite. 'Joss, the Home will have to be evacuated – and Quern must be prevented from using that weapon!'

'No, Keill.' Joss's voice was low but determined. 'The Veynaans may talk bravely of attacking, but Quern is certain that they will not dare. And no matter what happens – the Cluster will not back down!'

'Joss, you're wrong. Quern's wrong – if he really believes what he says. Just tell the Council that I'm coming in, with a message that their lives will depend on.'

'I'll tell them,' Joss said doubtfully. Then she added, 'Keill, how did you get here? What ship is that?'

He had been prepared for the question. 'Some kind of Veynaan ship. After Groll left me behind, I took it away from the men who came up to the satellite. Tell you about it later.'

He broke the connection, and turned his attention to landing as his ship hurtled down through the Cluster's yellow sky.

Skimming the upthrust crags of the rocks near the Home, he quickly found what he sought – the flat slope on the other side of the ridge where the Veynaan ship had attacked the ground-car, just after his arrival. Retros booming, landing jets screaming, in a cloud of billowing dust and flame he swept to a landing on the slope, hidden by the ridge from the Clusterhome beyond.

As he rose, Glr looked at him, a wistful, worried expression in the round eyes. He stroked her head reassuringly, wishing he could speak to her. Then he took an energy gun from his weapons compartment, clipped it to his belt and left the ship. Behind him, the airlock slid shut with a sound like finality.

At the Home, a crowd had gathered in the lower area. Nervousness as well as excitement sounded in the buzzing murmur that swept through them as Keill entered. No one spoke to him directly, but they fell back, making a passage for him as he strode quickly through, staring worriedly after him as he moved out of their sight up the spiral walkway.

In the corridor leading to the meeting room, Joss was waiting – pale and lovely, her dark eyes clouded with doubt and concern. She moved swiftly to him, her hands a feather-touch on his shoulders.

'Keill, I'm glad you're safe. But I'm not sure it was wise for you to come.'

'Maybe not,' he said. 'But I have to find a way to stop the insanity that you people have got yourselves into. Will the Council listen?'

'They'll listen – but I don't think you'll convince them.' She stepped away, and held out a hand. 'And, Keill – Quern has insisted that you shouldn't enter the meeting room armed. I have to ask you to give me your gun.'

Keill hesitated for only a moment. Speaking to the Council was the important thing. If the worst came to the worst, he knew he could deal with Quern as easily with his bare hands. He freed the gun from its belt-grip and handed it to Joss, then walked wordlessly into the meeting room.

As before, the Council sat at the long table, as if they had not moved since he was last there. The two old men seemed distinctly nervous, Fillon smouldered with ill-concealed anger, and even Shalet would not meet Keill's eyes. He was briefly grateful that, this time, Joss did not take her seat, but remained beside him, as if to lend her support to his words.

And, in the central seat, Quern was smiling.

'So glad to see you safe, Randor. Groll has felt the edge of my anger for his . . . hasty action.'

Keill looked at him silently, his eyes moving to the compact case of dark metal that the albino held, attached to a strap slung across his bony shoulders. No doubt it was the remote activator for the controls of the orbiting ultrafreighter, and its terrible cargo.

He swung his eyes to take in the rest of the Council. 'Joss

will have told you what I want to say. The Veynaans are going to attack the Cluster, before the time limit on your ultimatum runs out. Maybe any moment. And it won't be just a hit-and-run raid. They're coming in force to level the Home, to wipe you out.'

Fillon leaned back, sneering. 'Are you carrying messages from the Veynaans now?'

'My message is *about* the Veynaans, not from them,' Keill snapped. 'Listen to me! I'm trying to save your lives, and the lives of all the Clusterfolk!'

'Sounds more like you're trying to save the Veynaans!' Fillon spat.

'I'm trying to prevent more slaughter,' Keill replied. 'Slaughter that would horrify you – some of you – if you stopped to think about it.'

Beside him Joss stirred. 'You said *more* slaughter.'

'There were two hundred and thirty Veynaans on that planet Quern used to demonstrate your weapon on. An exploratory team. And I don't doubt Quern knew it.'

The others turned to the albino, shock registering on the faces of Shalet and the two old men.

Quern shrugged coldly. 'There are casualties in every war.'

'Casualties?' Keill said bitterly. 'You're sitting there with the power to murder *millions* of people – and you're planning to use it!'

Shalet interrupted, her broad face frightened. 'But Keill – Quern has said all along that the Veynaans'll give way, that the weapon won't ever be used.'

'And I say it again,' Quern put in. 'The Veynaans may make warlike noises among themselves, but they will not move against us.'

'Even if they do,' Fillon added darkly, 'we can't just run and hide and give them the victory. Not if we and our children are going to have the kind of future that we have been fighting for!'

Keill clenched his fists angrily. 'There will be no future, for any of you, if you give Quern his way. You must all see that. You must realize that Quern *wants* to use that weapon – just as he has been using your revolution. For his own insane, evil purposes!'

There was a blank, stunned silence. Then Fillon's lip curled again. 'That's an absurd statement. What are these purposes Quern is supposed to have?'

In that moment, Keill knew that he had lost them. He could not introduce into this gathering the truth about the Death-wing and its evil Master. He had no way of proving such statements – and even in making them he would be revealing more about himself, and why he was there, than he dared.

And Quern laughed. 'See, he has no answer.' He rose to his full height, the icy smile fading. 'We have listened to this foolishness long enough. To my mind, it is deeply suspicious. Here is Randor, returning in a ship that he admits is Veynaan, filled with wild tales about a Veynaan attack, seeking to undermine our courage, our will to win!' One skeletal white hand slapped down on the table. 'That, to me, is no less than treachery!'

A further silence fell. Keill glared round the table, but saw that even Shalet seemed confused and worried by Quern's words, while the faces of the others had hardened, as if convinced that the albino was right.

Quern cocked a white eyebrow, his mouth twisting in an acid, triumphant grin. And once again within Keill an incandescent fury began to build, channelled and controlled to feed the power that was on the verge of exploding. He poised himself to do what he had to do – the only alternative left to him.

'I haven't come to betray you,' he said, eyes blazing. 'I've come to save you from betrayal – and worse. And I will.'

His muscles tensed for the final leap at Quern's skinny throat. But in that instant he sensed movement behind and beside him. And he held back, trying to turn, to redirect his forward lunge.

He did not see the blow. But he felt it, like a sunburst in his head. Then he felt nothing more.

chapter ten

He awoke with what seemed to be laughter all around him, dying away as his consciousness returned. Deathwing laughter, cruel and gloating. Or perhaps, out of some nightmare, the laughter of death itself, drawing near – his own death, that of many Clusterfolk, the megadeaths of Veynaans.

He sat up carefully, letting dizziness and the pounding of his head subside. He was lying on a bunk in a cubicle – perhaps the same one that he had used before. The door was no doubt locked, and probably guarded, though no sound penetrated from the corridor outside. And he was manacled.

His hands and feet were embedded in two blocks of clear plastic, a familiar enough form of restraint on the Inhabited Worlds. The plastic would have been liquefied until his hands and feet had been placed within it – then a molecular hardener would have been added, to transform it into solid, unbreakable blocks. Somewhere there would be a key, a sonic device that would alter the stresses within the plastic and crumble it into dust. But he had no doubt that Quern would be in charge of the key.

His Legion training rallied, bringing a clear-minded calm to rinse away the frustration and fury that threatened to build within him. Coolly, he assessed his position.

He had failed, of course, completely. The Home would not have been evacuated, even though the Veynaan attack might come at any second. Quern was still fully in charge. And even Joss had turned against him, at the last – probably swayed by Quern's accusation of treachery, or driven by her own fierce dedication to the Cluster's aims.

Worst of all, he thought sourly, she had even hit him with his own gun. He might have done well to remember, sooner, how quickly she could move.

Look for positive factors, he told himself. But he knew they were few, and thin. At least Quern had allowed him to remain alive, for unknown reasons – though the plastic manacles reduced the value of that fact. And, more positively, Glr was nearby – though, again, she would not know what had happened and so would not know what action to take, until, perhaps, it was too late.

In a way, Keill thought, it's too bad I wasn't killed. Glr would have sensed that, and then she would have moved against Quern. Probably more effectively than I have.

He surveyed his surroundings – but could see nothing of use in the nearly empty cubicle. Pointlessly he strained every gram of his strength against the confining plastic. He rolled off the bunk and struck the cube that gripped his arms, in front of his body, fiercely against the floor, then against the metal base of the bunk. The hard plastic was not even scratched.

He lay still, his mind searching for even a hint of a possibility.

And the cubicle door opened.

Shalet came in. Gone was all the bluff cheeriness that was normal to the big woman. She seemed hunched, older. Worry had etched deeper lines in her broad face, and her clenched hands were trembling slightly.

Keill hoisted himself to a sitting position on the floor. 'How did you get in? Isn't there a guard?'

She nodded. 'Friend of mine. Told him official business.' Her mouth twisted. 'Maybe it is, too. Keill, I got to talk to you!'

'All right,' Keill said wryly. 'I'm not going anywhere.'

Shalet wrung her hands. 'I'm scared, that's what! Quern's been sayin' some funny things, actin' odd, ever since he got back last time. He acts – I dunno – he acts *hungry*, sort of, an' *eager*, like as if everythin' that's happenin' makes him real happy and excited. An' he's got that Groll doin' whatever he says, and Fillon – and Joss, too. You know she hit you?'

Keill nodded, grimacing.

'Whole Council's under his thumb now. 'Cept me, I guess. But I got to noticin', whenever Quern talked about what'd happen in the Cluster once we'd won, he started sayin' "I", not "we". As if he'll be runnin' things, alone. An' then when you came back, an' said what you did. . .' Her heavy jaw set solidly. 'I always had a good feelin' about you, Keill, an' I don't think you're a traitor!'

'Thanks for that,' Keill said quietly.

'An' I tell you what I do think – I think Quern's sick, that's what! I think he's out for power, like you said – an' doesn't care who he hurts, or how many he kills!'

'You don't know how right you are, Shalet,' Keill said. 'Do any other Clusterfolk feel like that?'

She shrugged. 'Dunno. Everybody knows what you said about the Veynaans comin' – you know how news gets round the Home. Lots of people have left – scattered out in the rocks somewhere, just in case. I'm thinkin' of goin', too. But I didn't want to leave you here. Quern said somethin' about havin' a lot of questions to ask you – an' he didn't look like he was goin' to ask them nice.'

'I can imagine.' Keill held up his plastic-encased hands. 'But how can you get me out?'

Shalet glanced over her shoulder at the door, then tugged something out of a pocket. Not a weapon, but a short, thin tube with an oddly shaped bulge at one end.

The sonic key.

Keill stared at it, amazed, then grinned at the grey-haired woman. 'Shalet, I could kiss you. How did you get it?'

She beamed. 'Groll had it – he was the one who put you in them things after Joss whacked you. I just told him I'd look after it, and he handed it over. After all, I'm still head of the Council – an' Groll's as stupid as he is big.'

'You're a genius.' Keill held out the manacles on his hands, Shalet raised the sonic key – then they both halted, listening.

The sky outside the Home seemed at once to be filled with a throbbing, rumbling roar – as if the grandfather of all thunderstorms was unleashing its wrath.

The massive building vibrated. It shook again, and again, as if pounded by some gigantic fist. The corridor beyond the cubicle filled with the sounds of plastiglass smashing, people screaming, the clatter of running feet.

'Keill!' Shalet yelled. 'The Veynaans!'

Beneath them the floor rippled and heaved. Shalet, ashen-faced, lost her balance, stumbled to her knees moaning in fright.

'Quick!' Keill's voice slashed across her hysteria like a whip, as he held up his trapped hands. Fumbling, weeping, Shalet brought the key into position. It made no sound above the violent tumult beyond the cubicle, but the plastic fell away, crumbling to powder.

He snatched the key, freed his legs, then sprang up, grasping Shalet's arm, dragging her roughly to her feet.

Then he flung open the cubicle door. The guard was standing in panic-stricken indecision, watching the terrified Clusterfolk pouring past him in a huddled, screaming mass. He began to turn as the cubicle door opened, but Keill effortlessly plucked the laserifle from his hands.

'Get out while you can, friend,' Keill said gently.

The guard looked around wildly, then turned and fled into the throng. Keill pulled Shalet out of the cubicle, thrusting the laserifle at her.

'Shalet, if these people panic completely, most of them will die inside the Home! They need direction now – they need you!'

The big woman steadied herself, eyes clearing, jaw setting firm. 'Right – I'm all right now.'

Keill gripped her shoulder in reassurance, then turned and plunged into the crowd. Behind him he heard Shalet's powerful voice booming, rising even above the thunderous, crashing explosions that spelled the end of the Home.

He moved through the packed, stampeding people with desperate speed, pushing, shouldering, dodging. At last he was on the walkway, springing up the deserted ascending spiral, ignoring the frenzied stream of people pouring down the descender.

He was remembering what Joss had said about the Council waiting in the meeting room for the Veynaan reply to the ultimatum. They might still be there, now that the Veynaans had replied with violence and death. He might still have a chance to stop Quern, and to save Joss and the others.

The upper levels of the Home were nearly empty when he reached them, and the wreckage more complete. Cracked and shattered walls, lumps of plasticrete flung from the Home's exterior, littered the corridor. But he did not slacken speed, sidestepping or hurdling the obstacles. Beneath him the floor leaped and bucked, like a living thing, as a heavy explosion nearby ripped at the building. But he kept his balance, hurtling through the meeting room's doors that hung twisted and askew.

Within was chaos and destruction. One wall of the room no longer existed, and smoking, half-molten rubble lay heaped on the floor where the table had stood. Keill feverishly kicked through the wreckage, but found only broken shards of the table. No bodies.

So all the Council had got out.

They might have tried to make it to the shuttles, he thought. Or they might have been on the descending walkway, among the crowds, even as he had rushed up the ascender.

But one way or another he knew that, as he stood there,

Quern might be pressing the switches that would murder a world.

He sprinted back to the walkway, ignoring the continuing blasts that tore at the fabric of the upper levels all around him. The descending walkway was nearly empty now, save for a few stragglers. And the lower levels were emptying fast, as the Clusterfolk streamed out of the many exits, away from their dying Home.

Outside, it was a scene from an inferno. Flame and smoke darkened the sky, the screams of terrified and injured people cut shrilly through the manic bellow of attacking spacecraft. Above the Home, the dart-shapes of a dozen Veynaan fighters wheeled and dived, energy beams slashing and pounding at the building. On the roof of the Home, a few remaining laser cannon bravely spat defiance – but even as Keill looked up, the whole of the two upper levels collapsed in a deafening eruption of smoke and dust.

And in the distance, Veynaan warships were settling on to the rocks, armed men in full battledress pouring from their airlocks as they touched down.

The Veynaans were landing on the far side of the basin where the Home stood, away from the ridge that sheltered his ship. If any Veynaan fighters had spotted his ship, it would have been a sitting target. But more likely the Veynaans were concentrating on levelling the Home. And Keill knew that Glr would wait for him until the very last minute – and, if necessary, longer.

He rounded a spur of rock, seeing that the Veynaan foot soldiers had rapidly moved closer, spreading their formation into a wide, sweeping, relentless curve. But some of the Clusterfolk were rallying, forming small pockets of resistance – tucking themselves into the shelter of the rocks, laserifles blazing at the attackers.

A group of such rifles was firing from an outcrop to Keill's right. Crouching, he moved towards them – and heard with pleased surprise the resonant voice of Shalet, directing the fire.

There were five in the group, including Shalet – their smoke-blackened faces set like stone with fierce determination. Shalet greeted Keill with a whoop of joy, and almost in the same instant dropped a Veynaan with a lancing beam from her rifle.

'Shalet, do you know what happened to Quern, or the others?'

She shook her head. 'Haven't seen 'em. I heard old Bennen was killed, in the Home – and Rint's out here somewhere, with a rifle. Don't know about Quern.' She fired again, missed, cursed richly. 'But somebody said one of the shuttles lifted off just before the Veynaans got here.'

The galling taste of failure rose in Keill again. He guessed that Quern had paid more heed to Keill's warning than the albino had been willing to admit, and had made his getaway – most likely taking Joss along.

It was past time, Keill thought dismally, to make his own getaway.

He glanced round the bulwark of the outcrop. The Veynaans were almost on them – and carrying hand beamers and energy guns, far more powerful than the out-dated lasers.

'You'll have to move, Shalet!' he shouted urgently. 'You'll be cut off in a couple of minutes!'

The big woman nodded and bellowed at her group. They slid down into a gully that ran beneath the outcrop, then hesitated.

'This way,' Keill barked. 'There's a good ridge not so far from here, and my ship is just beyond it. Let's move!'

Instinctively his voice had taken on the commanding tone of a Legion officer. As instinctively, the five formed up behind him, trotting obediently along as Keill moved ahead along the gully.

The wrinkled, creased slopes of the basin that contained

the Home produced plenty of gullies, furrows and shallow ravines, interspersed between its ridges and crests. These low areas offered shelter and a tangled network of paths that might take them near Keill's ship with a minimum of exposure.

And one quick glance around from the height of the outcrop had given Keill a picture of the terrain, now printed like a three-dimensional map on his mind's eye. He could see the twisting, mazy route that he must take as if it were a bright red meandering line on that map.

Urging Shalet and the others to greater speed, he raced ahead of them along that route, more and more desperate to get out of the basin, up on to the ridge where Glr was waiting.

But around a craggy shoulder of rock, where one gully intersected another, the way was blocked.

Two Veynaan soldiers, on the level floor of the gully, spun towards him, guns sweeping round.

Keill was still unarmed. But the Veynaan beams blasted nothing but rock behind him as he flung himself into a flat dive to one side, against the rough, sloping rock at the side of the gully.

His hands struck for an instant, and then he rebounded as if his arms were springs. The battering-ram impact of his boots flung the first Veynaan off his feet – and Keill followed through into a twisting roll, reaching for the first soldier's dropped gun as that of the second man spurted flame.

The beam blistered rock only centimetres away from Keill's rolling form, but the Veynaan had no second chance. Behind Keill, Shalet's laser fizzed, and the Veynaan dropped.

Keill sprang up, holding the first soldier's gun, grinning tautly at Shalet. 'I've got a lot to thank you for.'

Her echoing smile flashed. 'I reckon we're about even.' Then the smile faded to seriousness. 'Keill – that ship of yours. I reckon we ain't comin'.'

Keill looked surprised. Beyond the gully, the thunderous

fire of the Veynaan fighters had become only sporadic now. But the air was torn with the blazing crackle of energy guns, the shrieks of fleeing and dying people and scattered bursts of answering laser fire, as the Veynaan forces advanced upon the overwhelmingly outnumbered Clusterfolk.

Shalet shrugged. 'We ain't gonna win this fight, but we ain't gonna run from it either.' Her eyes misted slightly. 'I wish we'd listened to you. I wish we'd stopped Quern.'

'So do I.' He took her hand, groping for the right words to say. But the words never came.

Instead, a heart-stopping sound froze him in his tracks.

A scream. His own name, in a scream of pure agony and terror, drawn-out, weakening, trailing away.

And a scream that was silent. That was heard only in his mind.

Glr.

chapter eleven

Keill raced over the rocks like a blind, unstoppable projectile, arrowing in a perfectly straight line towards the steep ridge that hid his ship.

He had hardly been aware of Shalet's grunt of surprise as he had suddenly flung himself away, up the slope of the gully at top speed. He hardly looked at the crumbling, cracked, treacherous surface of the rocks beneath him, letting instinct and reflexes maintain his sure-footed balance. He was unaware of the occasional random energy beam that sizzled past him or splintered rock at his feet, as he sprinted across the furrowed terrain. He did not even think of the Veynaan gun that he had acquired, and that he had thrust into his belt at his back, to keep it out of the way during his half-crouched, headlong dash.

But for all his blazing speed, for all the unthinking cold fear and fury that gripped him, he was still a legionary. Though he leaped without slowing up the near slope of the ridge that he sought, he slid at once to a halt before reaching the top, and raised his head with slow caution to peer over the crest towards his ship.

It rested as he had left it. No Veynaan energy beam seemed to have been flung at it; no sound or sign of movement came from it.

But the ship had been landed so that the airlock was on the far side, not visible from where Keill crouched. He ghosted over the lip of the ridge, down the far slope, circling the ship.

The airlock was open, the landing ramp extended. And at the foot of the ramp stood a menacing, hulking figure.

Groll – with a laserifle levelled at Keill's chest, and a brutal smile twisting his thick lips.

'Master Quern said you'd be along.' The smile broadened. 'Always right, him.'

Groll could not have seen the Veynaan gun, in Keill's belt at the back. But Keill did not reach for it – did not respond directly in any way. Instead, the strength seemed to drain out of him. His head dropped, his shoulders slumped, his hands dangled limply at his sides. He stumbled slightly as he moved towards the ship.

Groll grinned cruelly at the visible signs of defeat. 'Took on more'n y' c'd handle, didn't y', legionary?' He motioned abruptly with the rifle towards the ramp. 'In y' go.'

Keill moved forward like a sleepwalker. Groll stepped aside, the rifle unwavering, as Keill reached the foot of the ramp. He took a plodding step up, then another. One more would bring him level with the watchful Groll, and the gun at Keill's back would be visible.

He began the next step, then seemed to stumble again, sagging forward.

Groll, chuckling coarsely, swung the rifle around, the heavy butt lashing out brutally to drive Keill forward.

But it missed its target.

In that fragment of time Keill's right hand blurred – reaching back, plucking the Veynaan gun from his belt, firing unerringly across his back.

And Groll's heavy body crashed backwards to the ground, his chest a smoking ruin.

Keill turned towards the airlock. But before he could take the four paces into his ship, a voice floated out to him from within.

A voice cold as death itself, tinged with laughter that bore an infinity of malice.

The voice of Quern.

'If that was your gun, Randor – and I'm sure it was –

throw it into the ship. And then follow it in *very* carefully. Or I shall turn this creature of yours into ashes.'

Keill scarcely hesitated. The gun went clattering in through the airlock, and he walked in after it, keeping his hands visible.

But as he stepped through the inner door, he stopped as if he had been struck. The blood congealed in his veins, his mind reeled.

Glr lay in a crumpled heap on top of the control panel.

She lay on her side, motionless, her hands limp, her eyes blank and sightless, her wings half-opened beneath her like crumpled leaves.

'Tricked you!' Quern's gloating laughter resounded from the bulkheads. 'It is already dead! And so will you be, legionary, if you move!'

Keill turned slowly, painfully, as if his muscles were strangers to him. Quern stood towards the rear of the ship's interior, a beam-gun levelled at Keill.

The albino's red eyes drilled into him, the manic laughter slashing like a whip. At once within Keill the numbness of shock gave way to a volcanic flood of killing fury. He was on the point of launching himself at Quern's throat, whatever the energy gun did to him in the process.

But Quern saw the blazing rage in Keill's eyes and took a nervous step backwards. As he did so, the black metal case slung round his shoulder clanged against the bulkhead.

And that sound sliced through Keill's torrential rage, and reawakened his control.

A still rational fragment of his mind drew conclusions. Quern was still carrying the weapon's activating mechanism; and he was here, not on the shuttle. So there was a chance, for reasons he could not guess, that the weapon had not yet been used.

'Move away!' Quern screamed. 'Over by the controls!'

Keill moved as he was directed. The glaring mists of his

fury began to clear, and his balanced, cool alertness was restored. There *will* be a chance, he told himself. To avenge Glr and save the planet, at once, will make victory the sweeter.

Quern's gloating smile returned as he saw Keill apparently submissive. He stepped forward, positioning himself near the airlock, the gun held firm. 'Now take the ship up,' he ordered. 'Gently – no tricks with acceleration!'

Keill bent silently over the small body of Glr, lifting her with care into her special sling-seat, smoothing the limp, delicate wings. Then, obediently, he slid into his own sling-seat and lifted the ship up into the Cluster's yellow sky.

'Excellent,' Quern snarled. 'The Veynaans may well pursue us, but you will be able to enter Overlight before they become dangerous. Set a course to emerge in deep space beyond Veynaa, on its far side.'

Keill's hands moved over the controls.

'I was naturally reluctant to perform the final act of this drama without being on hand to watch it,' Quern went on. 'And it was good of you to provide me with a ship, when the Veynaans destroyed the second shuttle. I had thought for a moment that I might not personally have the pleasure of pressing the switches.'

Keill said nothing, but a fierce triumph leaped within him. The planet *was* still unharmed.

'Indeed, everything has worked out better than I dared hope.' The laughter was a vicious giggle. 'When the Veynaans attacked so suddenly I feared that I had lost you. But I might have known you would find a way out. With Shalet's help, no doubt?'

Still silent, Keill puzzled over the vague but ominous meaning of Quern's words. But at least the albino, enjoying what seemed to be his victory, was talking freely.

'I thought you wanted to lose me,' he said, letting his voice seem dull, defeated.

'So you have not become speechless?' Quern sniggered.

'Excellent. No, you are quite important to me. When we have watched my little show, we will journey awhile together – and I will seek more of your conversation.'

In the viewscreens, as Keill's ship left atmosphere, the distant flares of a squad of Veynaan fighters, racing in pursuit, slid into view against the background of starry vastness. But within seconds, the screens blurred – and the views of deep space were replaced by the blank and empty nothingness of Overlight.

'Then you can tell me more about yourself, legionary,' Quern continued, grinning like a skull. 'And about *that*. A telepathic alien – fascinating. Regrettable that it resisted me, and that my mind-force was too powerful for it. I might have learned many interesting things from it.'

'And made The One very pleased,' Keill added quietly.

There was a hiss of surprise from Quern. 'So your "wing of death" remark was not coincidence,' he said, his voice icily thoughtful. 'More and more fascinating. A legionary who has survived the death of his world, who comes posing as a wrecked space drifter but has a ship containing a telepathic alien – and who knows more of the Deathwing and its leader than he has any right to know.' The red eyes studied Keill like a specimen on a slide. 'This mystery will intrigue the Master himself. The One is already looking forward to prying out your secrets.'

Something odd in that last remark tried to force itself on Keill's attention. But he was concentrating instead on the disturbing information that Quern had already contacted the Deathwing's nameless leader, and had passed on information about Keill.

Still, it had to happen sometime, he thought. He had been lucky in his first meeting with one of the Deathwing, who had not communicated with his leader before he died at Keill's hands. And in any case it would not matter. He had no intention of remaining the docile prisoner of the maniac who had murdered Glr.

Around him the viewscreens shimmered. The welcome reality of space sprang to life on the screens as the ship emerged from Overlight. Putting the controls on manual, Keill rotated the ship slowly – until a small, bright spheroid that was the planet Veynaa was fixed in the centre of the forward screen.

As he did so, his eye caught a small flare in the distant black depths, and recognized the planetary drive of another ship.

Quern had spotted it too. 'Ah, my little fail-safe seems to be in position.'

Keill understood at once. 'The shuttle?'

'Precisely. On its way to the freighter, to stand by. If anything had happened to me—' Quern grinned maliciously at Keill '—they would activate the weapon directly. As it is, when I press the switches, they will know at once, and will have time to get clear.'

Quern reached down to the metal case slung round his shoulders and flipped open the lid, to reveal rows of multicoloured switches.

Keill stirred, reaching for words, any words, to create a delay that might give him the opening he needed. 'What's going to happen, when you use those switches?'

The albino smirked. 'I wondered if you would be curious. And I am happy to enlighten you. Some of these switches will operate the freighter's controls, bringing it out of Overlight, altering its orbit. That will warn my fail-safe, to get clear. When the freighter is well into the Veynaan atmosphere, the container of the weapon will be opened – and its contents expelled. Then minute quantities of the radioactive substance will begin a reaction – sub-microscopic at first, accelerating at great speed into a chain reaction. It alters the very nature of the *air itself* – so that in moments the planet will be enveloped in a radioactivity that instantly and fatally enters the body of every air-breathing thing.' He giggled, horribly. 'As you will know, Randor, from having seen Moros.'

At the mention of his dead world's name, every scrap of

Keill's control was needed to keep him from leaping, suicidally, at Quern's throat. But he fought his fury again, and won. Coldly he said, 'What is this magical radioactivity? I know of no such substance.'

'If you did,' Quern tittered, 'you would be only the second in the galaxy to know – after myself.'

Keill blinked, taken aback by the implications. 'You mean that . . . *you* are. . .'

'The creator of the weapon, yes,' Quern announced, drawing himself up. 'I am a scientist, Randor, not a gunman. A *great* scientist. The radioactivity is my own discovery – and no one in the Deathwing, not the One, not the Master himself, can fathom the physics that led me to it. It is *mine*, legionary, mine alone!'

If that is true, Keill thought fiercely, then when you die, the secret of this monstrosity dies with you.

'Now,' Quern said, red eyes gleaming manically, 'let us proceed.'

Skeletal white fingers clawed over the switches. But the gun in the other hand did not quiver a millimetre. Desperately Keill sought a way to delay a moment longer, perhaps to make Quern forget himself, to make that gun muzzle waver – for just long enough.

'Are you really insane enough,' he asked harshly, 'to kill so many millions of people?'

Demonic anger flared in Quern's eyes. 'Insane? Small minds always see insanity when they look at a superior being!'

Keill shook his head. 'I have met superior beings, Quern. One of them lies there.' He gestured towards Glr's still form. 'Superior beings do not slaughter worlds. Only homicidal maniacs do.'

That, he knew, was the turning point, make or break. He was poised like a notched arrow, ready for the faintest opening that Quern might allow.

But Quern allowed none. Perhaps the prospect of destroying Veynaa gripped him too firmly to allow Keill's barbs to undermine his caution. The red eyes narrowed. Quern stepped away, his back to the airlock, putting more space between himself and Keill.

'I see,' he hissed. 'You wish to anger me, to make me careless. But you will not. I am ready for you, legionary.'

A bloodless finger curved over the gun's firing stud.

'Would you shoot me, Quern,' Keill said quickly, 'when the One wants me alive?'

'The Master's plan requires the destruction of Veynaa,' Quern snarled. 'Whatever secrets you might reveal are of secondary importance.'

Again, an oddness in the words nudged at Keill's awareness. But he could not focus on it. He was too overwhelmingly aware of the task he must perform.

Quern would not be diverted or thrown off balance. The gun remained rock-steady, and within seconds the switches would be thrown.

Keill knew that he would have to charge full into the muzzle of the gun – and would need all his speed and strength and will to stay alive long enough to get his hands on Quern.

And even then the planet would not be preserved – for Quern's 'fail-safe' in the shuttle would activate the weapon.

Even so, he thought grimly, it will be worth it. His death – and Glr's – would not be entirely meaningless. The Deathwing would not have a live Keill Randor to interrogate, putting the Overseers at risk. And the frightful weapon that was Quern's secret would be lost to the Warlord.

Quern was watching him coldly, the cruel smile twitching at his pale lips. 'Resign yourself, Randor. Be still, and watch the viewscreen. I only wish that I had time to bypass that strange barrier of yours – I would enjoy reading your inner reactions to what you are about to see.'

In the last instant before Keill flung himself suicidally at the albino, realization burst like a flare within him.

That was what had been so odd about those earlier remarks! Quern had spoken of prying out his secrets – and now of his 'barrier' – as if Keill's mind was still shielded!

Which could only mean . . .

But before he could complete the thought, Quern screamed.

He staggered backwards, screaming again, a thin shriek of pain. His face was contorted, the veins and cords of his neck jutting like ropes. The beam-gun dropped, harmlessly, and he clamped his hands as if in agony to his head.

Even before the gun landed, Keill was upon him.

He struck only once, with his fist. But every gram of his weight, every fraction of his towering fury, was released into that blow.

His fist crashed into the centre of Quern's white, screaming face. Bone splintered, blood spurted, masking the whiteness with red.

Quern's body was flung away, back against the inner door of the airlock. But – to Keill's astonishment – the door had opened, and the albino thudded limply into the airlock chamber.

Then the inner door closed – and before Keill could turn or move, the ship heeled violently to one side, throwing him off balance. The hiss of escaping air sounded unmistakeably from the opening of the airlock's outer door.

Then Keill righted himself and swung round – to be halted again, for a very different reason.

Glr was up, her great wings half-spread, her hands flickering over the ship's controls.

Above her, a viewscreen showed a glimpse of Quern's white, motionless body, drifting away into space, the activator dangling uselessly, trailed by the red, frozen crystals of his blood like a comet's tail.

Keill stared at Glr, speechless, as she turned to regard him with luminous round eyes.

'You were dead!' he whispered aloud.

Your thought is poorly formed, Glr said reprovingly. *Please stop gaping, and tell me what we must do next.*

chapter twelve

Keill slumped into his sling-seat, trying to focus his scrambled thoughts. *'Why did you let me think you were dead?'* he asked Glr, reproachfully.

I apologize for that, Glr said, sounding not at all apologetic. *But I could hardly lower my shields and reassure you.*

'You were shielding, all the time you were lying there, without Quern knowing?'

Certainly. My shielding, as I told you, seems too alien for human telepaths to recognize. They must see it as an absence of thought, a non-existence – easily confused with death.

As Keill shook his head, mystified as ever by the strange nature of telepathy, Glr went on to tell him what had happened.

Quern had arrived at Keill's ship only minutes after the Veynaan attack had begun. And as the albino had entered the ship, Glr had lowered her shields.

'Just like that?' Keill asked. *'When you knew how strong he was?'*

You had to be warned, Glr replied simply. *And he had to be stopped from lifting off, in your ship.*

But the moment that Glr's mind was open to him, Quern had hurled a ferocious psychic blast at her – then another and another. Under that terrible battering she knew that she could not survive for long, so she began rebuilding her mental shield – and Keill's – a little at a time.

To Quern it must have seemed that my mind was fading, dying, she said. *I let my wings flutter and droop, and when my shield was complete and my body still, he was sure he had killed me.*

'So was I,' Keill put in.

Your reaction made my portrayal all the more convincing, Glr said, with a smile in her voice. *Of course I left my eyes open, so I could see. And when it was plain that you were going to leap at Quern, despite his gun, I dropped my shield and struck him with the strongest mental blast I could muster.*

The images rose in Keill's mind – Quern's agonized screams, then the blood-masked body collapsing into the airlock . . .

An unpleasant death, Glr commented. *But well deserved.*

'It's not the end, though,' Keill said quickly.

As he told her about the others – Quern's fail-safe – he quickly scanned the viewscreens. The shuttle was out of visual range, but the sensors on the control panel revealed a tell-tale blip. The other ship was halfway round the planet from Keill's position.

It might already be at rendezvous with the freighter, he thought, and putting a stop to the huge ship's random dips in and out of Overlight. But there would still be time. Keill could hurl his own ship into Overlight, and arrive at the shuttle's present position in seconds.

He set the controls, and the viewscreens altered at once to the blank void of Overlight.

Can we stop them from activating the weapon? Glr asked.

'With luck,' Keill said. 'They're only on standby – they won't know Quern's dead, yet.'

They will know when you appear, Glr pointed out.

'But then,' Keill said fiercely, 'they won't have time to do anything about it.'

And do you know, Glr added, *who 'they' are?*

Keill's eyes darkened. 'I have a pretty good idea.'

As he spoke, the viewscreens shimmered. They were back in normal space – and ahead, outlined against the stars, was the dark cylinder of the ultrafreighter.

*

Keill slammed on full power, and his ship screamed down towards the huge ship. The shuttle had vanished, no doubt already within the freighter. But its occupants, not expecting to be pursued, had not altered the automatic action of the docking bay.

It slid obediently aside as Keill's ship approached, and he plunged into the opening, retros thundering, slamming his ship down jarringly on to the landing pad – next to the bulbous shape of the shuttle.

There was no sign around the pad of a human figure. For the necessary seconds Keill sat still, impatience struggling to overcome his control, while life support was restored in the freighter's stern compartment. At last his ship sensors showed that it was safe to go out. He sprang up, snatching another energy gun from his weapons store.

'*They'll be in the control room by now,*' he told Glr swiftly. '*Stay with the ship.*'

Keill . . . Glr began unhappily. But the airlock had opened, and he was gone.

Beyond the flame-scarred landing pad, one of the wheel-less, two-seater personnel carriers stood idle on the auto-magnetic strip. Keill leaped into it, slamming its starting lever ahead to send it forward. The carrier had only one forward speed – and impatience built to desperation within him as it trundled along with agonizing slowness.

He glanced over the edge of the trackway, down into the shadowy depths of the freighter. It was as empty as before, with a few work-robots still standing idle, arms drooping like the branches of dead trees.

It was likely, he thought, that one of the people from the shuttle would come back towards the launching pad, to investigate the arrival of a second ship. But there was only one way to come – along the suspended trackway of the vehicles which connected the landing pad and the control room.

Of course there was a flat hoist elevator at the landing pad, and another at the freighter's far end serving the control room, to give access to the deck of the cargo hold below. But no one would go down that way to investigate Keill's arrival. The trackway was too high, and an occupant of one of the carriers would be hidden from someone gazing upwards from the deck.

The small car slid onwards, passing through a doorway, automatically opened, in the first of the vast bulkheads that divided the freighter into sections. Ahead, the trackway remained empty, the hollow vault of the freighter silent. Then another bulkhead, another doorway . . .

And beyond, another of the carriers. On the parallel track next to Keill's, coming towards him, towards the landing pad.

Within it, the figure of a man – half-rising to his feet in alarm at the sight of Keill.

It was Fillon – pale and wide-eyed with startled panic, raising a hand that clutched the unmistakeable shape of an energy gun.

The gun in Fillon's hand crackled, but the beam flashed far over Keill's head.

The two cars trundled on towards each other.

'Fillon,' Keill shouted, 'Quern's dead – the rebellion is finished! It's over! Put the gun down!'

Fillon's answer was another wildly aimed shot, and another. Keill could see that the Clusterman's hand was shaking badly – yet the next shot bit into the trackway only half a metre from Keill's car, and the next sizzled not much farther away from Keill's right shoulder.

Keill crouched, eyes narrowed. The cars drew nearer, and still Fillon's gun blazed furiously, erratically but without pause.

As they drew closer, Keill knew that soon one of Fillon's blasts would be on target. His own gun flashed into his hand, and he snapped a shot without seeming to take aim.

But the beam struck just as he had intended, biting into Fillon's arm.

Fillon shrieked, lurching back. Yet somehow he did not drop the gun. He had been firing as he was hit, and the firing stud was still depressed as he fell back into the car, his injured arm jerking.

The lethal beam poured its power downwards, into the carrier Fillon was riding.

Keill heard the dull thud of an explosion within the machine. Then, like a blind, escaping animal, it veered suddenly to one side – and toppled over the edge of the trackway.

Fillon's thin, echoing scream was cut off when the carrier struck the metal deck of the freighter below, with a splintering, explosive crash.

Keill peered over the edge, as his own carrier neared the spot where Fillon had fallen. Below, what was left of Fillon's car lay in a heap of smoking, crumpled wreckage. It covered the lower half of Fillon's body – the upper half lying exposed, unmoving, eyes staring sightlessly upwards.

I wonder if you *were* a second Deathwing agent, Keill thought. Maybe I'll never know.

A moment more, and the carrier had reached its goal – a flat metal apron, as broad as the landing pad, outside the doorway that led to the control room in the freighter's nose.

Keill jerked the lever back, halting the carrier as it swung round into position for the return trip on the parallel magnetic strip.

Gun in hand, he sprang through the door.

The control room was narrow, cramped and unlovely, the metal coverings of the walls stained and dented with age. One of the meagre slits of the viewports was no longer clear plastiglass but a blank slab of metal – into which was set, like a plug, a shiny metal ovoid that Keill had seen before; in the container on the shuttle, during his secret visit to the roof of the Clusterhome.

The Deathwing weapon. The trailing hook-ups from one end of the ovoid now led into their connections within the freighter's control panel. The ovoid's other end would be jutting out through the port, ready, when activated, to spill its deadly capsules of radiation.

And at the control panel, across the open area from Keill, someone was standing. A small, slender figure in a bright Cluster coverall.

Joss.

As she turned to face Keill, she wore the same air of calm authority that she had shown on the first day they had met.

'I thought it would be you,' Keill said, just as calmly.

She studied him without expression. 'Fillon is dead?'

Keill nodded. 'And Quern as well.'

A frown creased the smooth brow, and anger flared in the dark eyes, quickly controlled. She glanced at the gun in Keill's hand. 'And are you going to kill me, too?'

'No.' Keill lowered the gun, returning it to his belt. 'But I'm not going to let you use the weapon, either.'

Joss backed away a step, leaning against the control panel. 'How will you stop me?'

'I hope you'll stop yourself,' Keill said. 'Think for a minute, Joss. I know how strongly you felt about the Cluster and its rebellion – but it's over now. The Veynaans have smashed the Home, and have probably taken the surviving Cluster-folk prisoner. There's nothing left!'

'Veynaa is left,' Joss said, her voice grating.

'But Veynaa means millions of innocent people,' Keill insisted. 'No matter how you feel, you can't commit murder on that scale, for revenge.'

'Quern told the Veynaans what would happen if they ignored our ultimatum,' Joss replied, determination drawing harsh lines on her face. 'Now it will happen!'

'Quern was insane,' Keill said sharply. 'He cared nothing for the Cluster. He belonged to an . . . an organization devoted to making war – and he was *using* you and the Clusterfolk. You can't use the weapon, Joss. That much evil makes everything it touches evil!'

To his surprise, Joss smiled. Not the warm, lovely smile he had seen so often before – but a thin, cold smile that held both mockery and triumph.

At the same moment, Keill felt a faint, throbbing vibration from the metal beneath his feet, heard a distant rumbling roar. The freighter's booster rockets, he realized, flaming into action to alter the giant ship's orbit.

'Joss . . .' he began, desperately casting about in his mind for the right words.

But she did not let him finish. With the speed that he had seen in her before, she swept her hand up towards him. It held a small, knobbled cylinder, covered with odd markings and tiny projections, like nothing Keill had seen before.

But he did not doubt that it was a weapon of some sort – and that Joss had caught him off-guard and flat-footed.

'Such a moving speech,' she smiled. 'But you have made it too late, legionary. And to the wrong person.'

She gestured with the cylinder. From behind him, Keill heard a slight grinding sound, almost muffled by the rumble of the boosters. He began to whirl.

But six powerful bands of shiny, flexible metal wrapped themselves round his body, pinning his arms to his sides.

chapter thirteen

Keill did not need to twist his head around to look. Another work-robot, he knew, with cold self-reproach. He had been too preoccupied with Joss to be properly alert, and the noise of the boosters had drowned the minimal noise of the robot's treads.

He tried to flex his arms, to seek some leverage within the steely grip. But the robot's six metal arms tightened round his body, and swung him up, off his feet. He was nearly immobilized, dangling as helpless as an animal awaiting slaughter.

Staring down into the cold and smoky eyes of Joss, seeing the demonic triumph that shone from her face, Keill wondered how he had ever thought her beautiful.

'You'll not smash this robot so easily,' she said, her mocking smile broadening.

'Then it was you – before – at the food tanks?' Keill spoke with difficulty as the robot's arms clamped ever tighter round his chest.

'Of course. You might have guessed. I told you I was a freighter pilot for the Cluster – and pilots learn to handle robots. With what Quern called a "delicate touch" – remember?'

Her laugh seemed almost metallic as she brandished the knobbly cylinder in her hand. And now Keill could guess its function – a remote manipulator for the robots.

He struggled again, lashing backwards with his boots. But he could not see, this time, the weak points to aim at, and his kicks glanced off the sturdy metal – while the unyielding bands around him tightened even further.

'I've set the robot controls to continue tightening its grip,' she said, still smiling. 'It will crush you to death in a few minutes. Meanwhile you may watch me complete the settings to activate the weapon – and then, when I've left you, you can pass the remaining time wondering which will kill you first – the robot or the radiation.'

'Can you kill ... so easily,' Keill gasped, 'so cold-bloodedly?'

Her eyes narrowed to icy slits. 'Easily?' she spat. 'I wanted you killed at the outset – I knew you would be a threat! But Quern would not hear of it. He insisted you were more valuable alive – he even reprimanded me for trying to kill you at the food tanks!' Her laugh was harsh, scornful. 'And now Quern is dead because he let you live – and I have been proved right. And when I have completed Quern's task, it will not be reprimands that I will receive!'

Keill stared down with chill horror at Joss's contorted, gleeful face, his mind half-numbed by the overwhelming truth that at last had been confirmed.

There *had* been a second Deathwing agent on the Cluster.

And he was looking at her.

He fought, in the robot's crushing grip, for breath enough to speak.

'Won't the One ... want me ... brought back for ... questioning?' he gasped.

Surprise and doubt flitted across Joss's face. 'How do you know so much?' she wondered, half to herself. 'Perhaps. . .' But then the look of cold determination returned. 'No – you will die. You have already disrupted the Master's plan enough, and you are too dangerous, as Quern found out.' A glint of anger flashed in her eyes. 'For that alone, the One himself would seek your death, if he were here. You have robbed the Master of his most valued weapon!'

That's something, at least, Keill thought, remembering

what Quern had revealed earlier, on the ship. No matter what happens now, the Warlord won't be murdering any more planets with that radiation. The secret of its making had died with Quern.

'Now our conversation must end,' Joss was saying. 'I have work to do – and soon the robot will crush your ribs, and put an end to your speeches.'

She turned away, laughing unpleasantly, towards the control panel.

Keill did not reply – but not because his ribs were crumbling under the robot's pressure. The increasing grip of the metal arms was painful, bruising the flesh of his arms and chest, but he pushed the pain to one side of his mind and ignored it, knowing that his bones could withstand stresses far more powerful than the robot could manage.

He calmed his mind, and formed the call. *'Glr – you'd better get up here. With a gun.'*

On my way, came the calm reply.

'*No – wait!*' An idea had sprung into Keill's mind – a way that he and Glr might thwart the Deathwing plan and still, with luck and speed, survive. *'Come in the ship! Burn your way through the bulkheads!'*

If you say so, Glr replied, with a faint note of puzzlement. *Are you aware that the orbit of the freighter is decaying?*

'*I know,*' Keill said quickly. *'How long before planetfall?'*

Your ship computer estimates four minutes.

And the weapon, Keill knew, would be activated before that – to release the radiation capsules into Veynaa's atmosphere, beginning the catastrophic chain reaction that would eventually leave nothing alive on the planet's surface.

'*Then hurry!*' Keill called, in silent desperation.

Two bulkheads remaining, Glr replied, as calm as ever.

Joss stepped away from the control panel, looking up at Keill, her eyes glittering. He let his body sag in the robot's grip, as if near death. And her smile was ugly – a distant echo of Quern's twisted gloating.

'If you can still hear me,' she said, 'it might brighten your final moments to know what is to happen. In about three minutes the container will open, and the radiation capsules will spill out.' She gestured towards the metal ovoid fixed in the viewport. 'But in one minute from now I will be back in the shuttle – or perhaps in *your* ship, if it is more suitable – and on my way to deep space. To watch Veynaa's death, and yours, from safety.'

She laughed mockingly, flung the robot control cylinder on to the control panel, and turned towards the door of the control room.

But then she paused. A new sound had begun to emerge from the bowels of the great freighter's shell. A crackling roar that was far louder and more powerful than the thrum of the boosters.

Glr – blasting her way through the nearest bulkhead with the energy guns of Keill's ship.

'What . . .' Joss muttered.

The roar outside grew to a bellow. Not of the guns now, but of the ship's retros. Keill twisted his head around, seeing the reflected orange flare of flame through the doorway as Glr swept the ship thunderously down on to the broad metal apron beyond the control room.

Paling, Joss whirled and sprang towards Keill, her hand clutching for the gun at his belt. But the robot's grip had pressed Keill's arm to his side covering the gun, and she could not work it loose.

Then Glr was in the room.

Wings booming, fangs bared, she seemed to fill the air above them, like some furious, blazing-eyed spirit of vengeance.

Joss screamed and cowered away. And in one of Glr's small hands an energy gun flashed and crackled.

The beam struck into the centre of the robot's pyramidal body. Smoke gushed from the wrecked circuits, and the robot jerked, its arms straightening, flying uncontrollably apart.

Glr hovered overhead, as Keill, released, dropped to the floor on his feet, before the terrified woman.

For a flashing instant he locked eyes with her, the deadly weapons of his hands poised like blades.

Then, with an inner snarl at his own weakness, he flung her aside with a sweep of his arm. Her slim body slammed brutally against the solid metal of the robot's body. And she crumpled, half-unconscious, to the floor as the robot, out of control, flailed its arms crazily through the air above her.

Ignoring it and Joss, Keill sprang to the control panel. As he moved, his mind was forming words with rigid concentration.

'Glr, get back to the ship and get ready to lift off! I'm setting the freighter for Overlight in thirty seconds!'

But . . . Glr began.

'Don't argue – go!' Keill yelled.

The great wings swept once, and Glr vanished through the door. Keill's hands were blurs as he made the adjustments to the freighter controls.

Then a scream of manic rage from behind him made him whirl, poised to strike.

There was no need. Joss had recovered and regained her feet, and may have intended to hurl herself at Keill, to prevent him altering the control settings.

But she had been prevented.

Perhaps it was the impact of Joss's body that had restored at least a few of the connections in the robot's damaged circuits. Enough to reawaken it to its most recent instructions.

Its whipping, threshing, steely arms had found Joss as she had risen.

Instantly they had clamped round her body, as they had around Keill's, and jerked her up off her feet.

She hung, suspended, struggling faintly. The robot's instructions had included an order to increase its pressure – and mindlessly it was obeying. As Joss saw Keill spin to look at her, the fear and fury drained from her eyes. Only a desperate pleading remained in their dark depths.

'Keill . . .' she whispered. 'Please . . .'

He glanced at the cylindrical control mechanism, on the control panel where Joss had thrown it.

Within his mind, the time-count that he had begun, when the freighter's controls were set, ticked relentlessly ahead.

Twenty-four seconds left . . .

He looked back at Joss, his face expressionless. 'I don't know how to operate the robot,' he said stonily. 'And there's no time to learn.'

Her scream was little more than a whimper as he turned away towards the control room door.

Outside, his ship waited on the platform, airlock open. He dived through, sprang to his sling-seat.

Nineteen seconds . . .

The ship's drive thundered into life. It lifted slightly. '*Now*', he said fiercely to Glr, '*a way out.*'

The ship's forward guns blasted. On the side of the freighter, metal glowed, began to flow down the curving sweep of the hull.

Thirteen seconds . . .

A hole appeared in the hull. Through it he could see more flame flickering – from the heat of the freighter's entrance into Veynaa's atmosphere.

Even before the hole was wide enough, he slammed on full power.

Nine seconds . . .

The ship screamed forward, guns still blazing. Its blunt nose smashed into the gap in the hull. In a rending explosion of tormented, half-melted metal, it burst through, and clear.

Six seconds . . .

Brutally Keill dragged the ship howling upwards, curving it away from the plummeting freighter. The Overlight field, when it was operating, extended out around a ship. He had to get well away.

Three seconds . . .

He glanced at his viewscreens, his ship still at full power. Just about . . .

Now.

In the screen, the image of the freighter blurred, shimmered.

Then it was gone.

Keill. Glr's inner voice was soft, worried. *You know that entering Overlight so near a planet can distort the field. The freighter could emerge anywhere – with the weapon.*

'It won't,' Keill said bleakly. 'I didn't programme it to emerge at all.'

And his ship climbed away towards deep space – while below, the planet Veynaa rolled peacefully on its axis, unheeding, unharmed.

Aftermath

chapter fourteen

In the distant, boundless expanses of deep space, in a sector of the Inhabited Galaxy where probably no one had ever heard of Veynaa or the Cluster, Keill's ship winked into existence out of Overlight.

At the controls, Keill ran his eyes again over the settings and computer data, confirming his course, then switched to automatic and leaned back, stretching luxuriously. Beside him, in her special seat, Glr also stretched, flaring her delicate wings.

Keill looked at her expectantly. She had been silent for a long time, reaching across the galaxy's distances to the minds of the Overseers in their hidden asteroid – reporting the final events over Veynaa, the ultimate defeat of the Warlord's plan.

Now awareness had returned to the bright round eyes that she fixed on Keill.

The Overseers are pleased, she announced. *All in all, they feel that we have been successful.*

'All in all?' Keill echoed, raising an eyebrow.

They do have certain regrets, Glr went on. *First, the Deathwing now knows that you exist, and that you are a threat to the Warlord's plans. Second, we have learned little more about the Deathwing, or its leader, or the Warlord himself.*

Keill snorted. 'I was a little short of time to have a long informative chat with Quern. Even if he would have told me anything.'

I put that point to the Overseers – somewhat forcefully, Glr said. Quiet laughter curled for a moment around her silent voice. *They then reported that peace has returned to the Cluster. The*

Overseers have indirectly encouraged a rumour on Veynaa that the Cluster rebellion was the fault of one unscrupulous, power-hungry leader, who is now dead.

'Accurate enough, as far as it goes,' Keill put in.

As you say. But because of this, the Veynaans are not being vindictive. The Cluster survivors have begun to rebuild their Home, and Veynaa has agreed to hold talks about improving their conditions and giving them more control over their lives.

'If that had happened in the first place,' Keill said sourly, 'Quern would never have got a grip on the Cluster.'

Humans are renowned, said Glr, *for perceiving the proper course of action when it is far too late to take it.*

'But it's not too late,' Keill objected. 'Not for the survivors, or the Veynaans. It would have been too late only if that weapon had been used.'

Agreed, Glr replied. *You will also be amused to know, from the Overseers, that the Veynaans are very pleased with themselves. They say that they were proved right – that the Cluster was bluffing, and did not dare to use such a weapon against an inhabited planet.*

Keill shivered, remembering how close it had been, how few seconds had remained before those deadly capsules would have spilled out into Veynaa's atmosphere.

And that thought recalled another that had been troubling him.

'Glr, what about the weapon?' he asked. 'The radiation capsules were still set to be ejected, which means they'd leave the freighter in Overlight.'

There is no danger. The capsules, as Quern told you, would react only on air – so the chain reaction cannot begin in Overlight. The capsules will remain harmless, outside the freighter but within the Overlight field, for eternity.

Keill did not reply, silenced by the awesome weight of that last word. Eternity.

My race, the Ehrlil, Glr went on, *has travelled longer and farther in Overlight than any humans, yet even we have fathomed only* a fragment of its nature. But we do know that a ship entering Overlight has entered a nothingness all of its own. It no longer inhabits 'normal' reality – but also it cannot impinge even on other ships in Overlight. In practical terms, the freighter simply no longer exists. Nor does the weapon. She paused. Nor does the woman.

Keill nodded sombrely. 'I see that. Anyway, the robot's grip would have killed her before long.' His eyes grew dark. 'And I don't think I would have released her even if I'd known how.'

For a few moments they sat silent, each wrapped in separate thoughts, not for communication. Then Glr stirred, shaking out her wings, looking around at the viewscreens.

You still have not told me what course you have set, she said brightly.

Keill responded to the change of mood, sitting up, glancing again over the control panel. 'I'm keeping a promise to you.'

A promise? Glr's eyes glowed. About the place where you say there will be good flying – where I may stretch my wings at last?

'I thought you'd remember,' Keill smiled. 'We'll reach the system soon that contains the planet I'm thinking of. It has a very small population in terms of land area – so there are huge tracts of it still totally untouched. In those regions there are places where the sun is warm, the turf is soft underfoot, and there are deep pools of the clearest water you'll ever see.'

No doubt that would be of great interest, Glr said loftily, to fishes and humans and other inferior species.

Keill laughed aloud. 'And beyond those pools,' he continued, 'are mountains that seem to reach up for ever, where strong winds blow all the time around the peaks, and the air is the freshest in the galaxy.'

Perfection! Glr cried. Her wings thrummed, her round eyes glistened. Can you not get more speed out of this primitive craft of yours?

And her silent, bubbling laughter mingled with Keill's as he reached towards the controls.

Douglas Hill
Galactic Warlord £1.25

He stands alone . . . his planet, Moros, destroyed by unknown
forces. His one vow – to wreak terrible vengeance on the
sinister enemy. But Keill Randor, the Last Legionary, cannot
conceive the evil force he will unleash in his crusade against
the Warlord and his murderous army, the Deathwing.

edited by Douglas Hill
Alien Worlds £1.25

stories of adventure on other planets

C. S. Lewis, Ray Bradbury, Arthur C. Clarke, Bob Shaw,
Robert Silverberg, John Brunner and Carol Emshwiller bring
you a marvellous collection of science fiction stories. Heart-
stopping adventure, horror, and the unexpected all affect our
galactic travellers.

Michael and his parents visit Mars for a holiday – then the
explosions start and they're trapped! Will they have to stay on
Mars for ever? And wait for the dead Martians to live again?

Aidan Chambers
Great Ghosts of the World £1.25

Feel the fingers of fear creep up your spine as you read these
tales of the supernatural. Vampires, devils, ghosts, bunyips,
poltergeists – from the ends of the earth come creatures of
nightmares to haunt you, taunt you and terrify you . .

Older Piccolo fiction you will enjoy

○	**Deenie**		£1.25p
○	**It's Not the End of the World**	Judy Blume	£1.00p
○	**Tiger Eyes**		£1.25p
○	**The Circus of Adventure**	Enid Blyton	£1.00p
○	**The Ship of Adventure**		£1.00p
○	**Scottish Hauntings**	Grant Campbell	£1.10p
○	**The Gruesome Book**	Ramsey Campbell	£1.00p
○	**Blue Baccy**		£1.25p
○	**Go Tell it to Mrs Golightly**		£1.25p
○	**Matty Doolin**	Catherine Cookson	£1.25p
○	**Mrs Flannagan's Trumpet**		£1.25p
○	**Our John Willie**		£1.25p
○	**The Animals of Farthing Wood**	Colin Dann	£1.75p
○	**The Borribles**	Michael de Larrabeiti	£1.50p
○	**Goodnight Stories**	Meryl Doney	£1.25p
○	**The Vikings**	Mikael Esping	£1.00p
○	**This School is Driving Me Crazy**	Nat Hentoff	95p
○	**Alien Worlds**		95p
○	**Day of the Starwind**		£1.10p
○	**Deathwing over Veynaa**		95p
○	**Galactic Warlord**	Douglas Hill	£1.25p
○	**The Huntsman**		£1.25p
○	**Planet of the Warlord**		95p
○	**The Young Legionary**		95p
○	**Coyote the Trickster**	Douglas Hill and Gail Robinson	95p
○	**Haunted Houseful**	Alfred Hitchcock	£1.10p

O **A Pistol in Greenyards**	} Mollie Hunter	£1.25p
O **The Stronghold**		£1.25p
O **Which Witch?**	Eva Ibbotson	£1.25p
O **Astercote**	Penelope Lively	£1.25p
O **The Children's Book of Comic Verse**	Christopher Logue	£1.25p
O **Owls in the Family**	Farley Mowat	50p
O **Gangsters, Ghosts and Dragonflies**	Brian Patten	£1.50p
O **The Cats**	Joan Phipson	£1.25p
O **The Yearling**	M. K. Rawlings	£1.50p
O **The Red Pony**	John Steinbeck	£1.25p
O **The Story Spirts**	A. Williams-Ellis	£1.25p

All these books are available at your local bookshop or newsagent, or can be ordered direct from the publisher. Indicate the number of copies required and fill in the form below   11

....

Name_____
(Block letters please)

Address_____

_____

Send to CS Department, Pan Books Ltd,
PO Box 40, Basingstoke, Hants
Please enclose remittance to the value of the cover price plus:
35p for the first book plus 15p per copy for each additional book
ordered to a maximum charge of £1.25 to cover postage and
packing
Applicable only in the UK

While every effort is made to keep prices low, it is sometimes
necessary to increase prices at short notice. Pan Books reserve the
right to show on covers and charge new retail prices which may
differ from those advertised in the text or elsewhere